A PUBLIS

To my dearest readers:

Triple Crown Publications provides you with the best reads in hip-hop fiction. Each novel is hand-selected in its purest form with you, the reader, in mind. *Let That Be the Reason*, an insta-classic, pioneered the hip-hop genre. Always innovative, you can count on Triple Crown's growth: manuscript notes — published books — audio — film.

Triple Crown has also gone international, with novels distributed around the globe. In Tokyo, the books have been translated into Japanese. Triple Crown's revolutionary brand has garnered attention from prominent news media, with features in ABC News, The New York Times, Newsweek, MTV, Publisher's Weekly, The Boston Globe, Vibe, Essence, Entrepreneur Magazine, Inc Magazine, Black Enterprise Magazine, The Washington Post, Millionaire Blueprints Magazine and Writer's Digest, just to name a few. I recently earned Ball State University's Ascent Award for Entrepreneurial Business Excellence and was named by Book Magazine as one of publishing's 50 most influential women. Those prestigious honors have taken me from street corner to boardroom accreditation.

Undisputedly, Triple Crown is the leader of the urban fiction renaissance, boasting more than one million sizzling books sold and counting…

Without you, our readers, there is no us,

Vickie Stringer
Publisher

China Doll

BY

Leah Branch

Compilation and Introduction copyright © 2010 by
Triple Crown Publications
PO Box 247378
Columbus, Ohio 43224
www.TripleCrownPublications.com

Library of Congress Control Number: 2010920094
ISBN 13: 978-0-9825888-0-2

Author: Leah Branch
Graphics Design: Valerie Thompson, Leap Graphics
Photography: Treagen Kier
Editor-in-Chief: Vickie Stringer
Editor: Maxine Thompson
Editorial Assistants: Christina Carter and Matthew Allan Roberson

First Trade Paperback Edition Printing 2010

10 9 8 7 6 5 4 3 2 1

Printed in the United States of America

Dedication

I first want to thank God for blessing me with
this gift, and the people He chose to surround me
with who have shown unwavering support.

Monique, thank you for walking through this with me every
step of the way and constantly reminding me to stay on
track. Jermol, thank you for seeing my abilities even when
I couldn't see them with my own eyes. I am truly grateful.

PART I

Chapter One

China
Dell

Proposal

"When is the food gonna be done? I'm starving over here, China," Teri said as she rubbed her belly.

"If you keep botherin' me, you ain't gonna get any. I need silence while I create," China teased, smiling.

Across from Teri sat her cousin Angie, who was nimbly filing her nails in silence. She raised an eyebrow at the comment, but knew better than to distract China from her culinary ambitions.

"Tonight we're eating fried chicken, greens, mashed potatoes, homemade gravy and cornbread." The menu took China right back to her childhood in Atlanta, but her thoughts didn't linger there for long. Every time she thought about her childhood, she got glimpses of abuse, both mental and physical, that she suffered by the hand of her mother, Myra.

The last time she'd seen her mother was in college, when Myra showed up at her dorm room, cursing and spitting at China. That was the last time China saw her, four years previous. She had no interest in a relationship with her mother since that day.

China pushed those painful thoughts from her mind.

"So I think Jag's coming over later, sometime after dinner."

"Oh, girl," Teri squealed.

"You know you gotta give us the lowdown on this guy," Angie added. "He is fine," she said, drawing out the word "fine" to make her point.

"Lowdown? There ain't no lowdown. He's just some guy," China said with a smirk. "Ok, y'all know me too well. I don't know – we've been dating for almost eight months. I like him, he treats me right."

"I bet he does," Teri said with a raised eyebrow, elbowing Angie in the ribs, laughing.

China Doll

"Well, yes, he does take care of business, it's just," China closed her eyes and took a deep breath, "I don't know. Shit. I think I wanna keep him one around for a while."

"Who knew a ride home would've ended up like this?" Angie said.

"Hell, I'd take him for a ride," Teri said, cackling at China.

"Girl, you nasty. You'd best keep your hands off though. Seriously, I'm standing around at the bus stop, and this fine-ass man just rolls up and decides he wants to give me a ride home? I didn't even have my hair done that day."

"Well, you always look good, China," Angie said.

China did always look good – supple, buttery skin that glistened, dark flowing hair down to the middle of her back and amber eyes that slanted upward a bit. Her eyes were the marked feature that earned her namesake when she was just a baby. When she emerged from her mother, those slightly upturned eyes made her mother exclaim "she's like a little China Doll." The name stuck.

"That's right. I'm sure he just wanted to take you home," Teri said. China detected a hint of jealousy in her tone.

"Don't hate. All I can say is, this man's taking care of me better than any man ever has – and I don't just mean in the bedroom," she said, winking at Angie.

At that moment, China pulled the chicken out of the fryer and started plating dinner for her friends.

"So what do y'all feel like doin' tonight? Let's go get into some trouble," Teri said.

"Girl I don't know, I already told you, Jag's comin' over," China sighed.

"I get it, I get it, whatever. I feel like goin' out and gettin' some kind of lovin'.'"

"You would," Angie said, looking Teri straight in the face and laughing. "You always do!"

The three women, all deeply attractive in their own way, sat at the table and laughed and talked through dinner. After an hour and a half, the ladies finished up and started gathering their things to leave China to get ready for her man.

China Doll

"Alright girls, call me tomorrow. We'll have to get into somethin' good, a club downtown or somethin'," China said, hugging Angie.

"You know it girl. I'll hit you up after work."

China closed the door after Teri and Angie left the small apartment and headed to the bathroom and turned the faucet on. She needed to get the smell of fried chicken and greens off of her and get ready for Jag. She hadn't seen him for two days and was starting to get anxious. It was summertime and the block was hot – so Jag wasn't about to let his hustle suffer. He'd made a few grand in the past two days, making sure to check in with China every night with a phone call when he could brag about everything that happened that day.

China stepped into the hot water and thick steam of the shower. She put her hair up in a tight ponytail to keep it from getting too wet and slowly lathered soap all over her skin – which was looking more and more perfect as the years went by. Every year, China seemed to become more and more attractive. The older she was, the more precious she became.

When she was done showering, feeling refreshed, she stepped into a pair of light pink, satin panties and a matching bra before slinking down onto the couch. She was sending a clear message: she was ready for her man.

China sat in front of her television, sipping red wine, until she heard three light taps at the door. She knew that knock, and immediately knew it was Jag.

She stepped to the door and slowly opened it, revealing her tight body inch by inch as the door swung open.

"Damn, girl," Jag said slowly, licking his lips. "What's all this about?"

China waited a moment to take it all in. She batted her eyelashes and looked deep into Jag's eyes before placing one index finger on his chest and slowly moving it downward until she found his belt buckle, grabbing it firmly.

"I'm not sure what you mean, baby," China said, with a playful smile.

Jag stood nearly two feet taller than China, with broad shoulders, a sharp jaw line, deep brown eyes and a brilliant smile. He knew he was attractive, but so did China. They made an amazing couple.

China leaned forward and got on her tiptoes. "You gonna come inside, or leave me waiting all day?" she whispered.

"I don't never leave my dime piece waitin'," he responded.

Jag took three steps inside, shutting the front door behind him.

"Smells good in here, girl. You been cookin'?"

China
Doll

"Of course I have. I just hope you're ready to work up an appetite."

Jag blinked and slowly shook his head back and forth. He knew she had game for days.

Jag put his large, powerful hand on the small of China's back, pulling her close.

"I got you somethin'" he whispered.

"What's that?" she asked, tilting her head back and slightly to the left. Jag reached into his pocket and pulled out a small, charcoal grey velvet box.

"Just a little somethin' somethin' for my girl."

China took the box in her hand and opened it slowly. As soon as she opened it, she realized that this wasn't any normal gift. Jag could see the diamonds reflecting in her eyes.

"Oh my god," she breathed, "this must have cost a fortune."

"Only the best for my baby," he said, and turned her around. He removed the diamond necklace from its box as she held her hair above her head. He fastened the clip around her neck and then kissed her earlobe.

China
Doll

"My baby," he whispered.

"Oh my God, I must be the luckiest bitch in Baltimore," China mused, throwing her arms around Jag. Before she knew it, he was backing her up into the kitchen, using one arm to clear off the kitchen counter behind her.

"I want you so bad," China said, breathing heavily.

"Oh yeah?" Jag asked, "tell me how bad."

"I want you to fuck me," China demanded, as she slid her hand into the front of Jag's pants.

"Oh, girl, you best say the magic word," he said, licking her lower lip.

"Please, daddy, fuck me!" she said through clenched teeth.

At that point, Jag dropped his pants and pulled his impressive member out, slapping it against China's bellybutton.

"Put that dick in me," China said.

"Oh yeah?" Jag teased, "You want it?"

China smiled and shook her head. Then, Jag picked her up, palmed her ass and went deep into her, hitting her G-spot with the first thrust.

"Damn, boy, you know just how to hit it, don't you?" she almost had tears in her eyes. Jag lifted her up again and turned around, putting her back against the wall while her legs were still in the air. He started pounding her for all she was worth, and China loved every second of it.

"Shit! Get it boy! Damn!" she screamed. "If you keep fuckin' me like this, I'm gonna come!"

"Do it baby," he said, "come for me," just then, a shockwave went through China's whole body, a surge that made her scream out.

"Jag!" she moaned, "Holy shit I'm coming!"

Jag intensified his pace, and over the next minute, China climaxed three more times. After the fourth, Jag's eyes rolled back into his head.

"Damn girl, my turn," he said, gritting his teeth. He pulled out and busted his nut all over China's stomach. "Shit," he panted, "you a bad ass bitch."

They looked at each other for a few seconds before Jag picked China up and walked toward the bedroom. He put her right into bed and then plopped down right beside her. China was all too familiar with this position, so she placed her head on his chest like she always did.

"China," Jag said hesitantly, "I, I wanna tell you somethin'," he took a deep breath.

"Baby, don't say nothin', you don't need to" China said, almost out of breath.

"No girl, I been tryin' to keep it deep down, but I gotta say it. I feel like it's been eatin' me alive."

China stopped being aloof and looked at Jag as if something serious were about to happen.

"Baby, what's up?"

"Well, you know we been seein' each other for about,

what, eight months now?"

"Yeah," she smiled. She was a little surprised he actually remembered.

"Well, you know I get around the block a lot, and no other girl even comes close to you. You got a job, with your head right, your own place, you're fine as hell and you can cook," he laughed a few times at himself. "I know it sounds lame but," his voice trailed off. "I don't know, never mind."

"But what?" China said, getting a little loud for such a tender moment.

"Nothin', I'm just bein' stupid," Jag said, shrugging.

"No, baby. What's up? Talk to me."

Jag took a deep breath and looked China right in the face.

"I fuckin' love you, China."

Those words hit China like a garbage truck. No one had said those words to China since her father died.

"You, you love me?" China asked.

"Aw, see? Shit! I knew I shouldn't be comin' over here shootin' my mouth off expectin' you to–" China cut him off, putting a finger to his lips.

"Shut up." She said.

"I love you too, baby." She said, and took her finger from his plump lips.

Jag half smiled. "Well good, cause if you laughed at me, I wouldn't know what to do."

China grinned.

Jag stood up and walked toward the kitchen, returning a few seconds later.

"Well, since all our shit's on the table, I might as well do this. I was gonna wait until our one-year anniversary, but fuck it. Might as well do it now. You only live once." China didn't understand what he was talking about.

"Only live once? Baby, what? You ain't dying," she said, laughing.

"It ain't even about that," he said as he leaned down

toward the bed. "Will you marry me?"

One tear streaked down China's face as she tried to form the right words – words that wouldn't come out.

"Are you, are you serious?" China asked.

"China, I ain't gonna ask you again," Jag said, teasing.

"Yes," China screamed, "Yes! Yes!"

China
Doll

Chapter Two

Making Moves

The first thing China did when she woke up the next morning was three-way call Teri and Angie so she could relay the news to her best friends at the same time. As soon as she said the word "proposed" through the telephone receiver, there were a few seconds of silence before both of her friends erupted into high-pitched squeals. "Oh my God!" they screamed in unison.

In the days that followed, they went into in full-tilt wedding mode. They talked about everything: wedding magazines, hairstyle ideas, locations and bridesmaid's dresses.

"I can't help but feel like I'm in a damn fairytale," China said to Angie one night over the telephone.

"You need me to come over there and pinch you?" Angie said with an attitude.

"I don't even know, girl. I just can't believe it. I've never felt this way about a guy before, and you know I've had a few in the past," China said, chuckling to herself about her exploits in college.

"You just caught nerves. Just go with it, China. If you love Jag like you say you do, you ain't got a damn thing to worry about."

"You're probably right. That's why I keep you around. You check my ass," China said.

"You're my girl! That's what I'm here for. Reality Check!" Angie laughed

"OK, well, it's about time I get off the phone, I've got a big day tomorrow. I gotta get to bed early," China said, yawning. She knew everything was on track, but she couldn't help but feeling like a bad moon was rising. She'd never been this lucky in love – in her career – in her life. She had a sneaking suspicion that ate away at her, usually right before bed, but tonight, she pushed her fears out of her mind and went to sleep.

᎗ ᎗ ᎗ ᎗ ᎗ ᎗ ᎗ ᎗ ᎗ ᎗ ᎗ ᎗ ᎗ ᎗ ᎗ ᎗

A few hours later, in the middle of the night, she heard a knock at her door. She sat straight up in bed and walked to the door and looked through the peephole. It was Jag.

"Jag!" she said as she opened the door.

"Hey baby," he said, as he took a step in and lifted China off of her feet.

"You're sure in a good mood," China said, suspiciously.

"I made some moves tonight," he said proudly. China wasn't completely ignorant about street life, she knew that he was implying he made some major cash – cash that probably wasn't made in the most wholesome way.

"These niggas was in town from DC, running their mouths like they knew shit."

China didn't like the sound of where this was going. Things like this never ended well.

"So me and my boys took 'em for everything they were worth. Stripped the cash, and flipped all the coke the were holdin' in just a few hours." He looked satisfied with himself, like a wild-west bandit who just got away with a holdup, scot free.

"Who were they?" China asked. Jag looked at her like she'd crossed a line. She didn't need to get that deep into the details of his business.

"Some small time niggas. Who the fuck cares. What matters is that I'm gonna put all that cash into your wedding. I'm gonna make you a queen, China."

"I'd like that. So, you gonna give me that big ol' wedding that every girl has ever wanted, and we'll invite everyone we know?" China asked.

"Yeah. Well, not everyone," Jag paused, "I don't want those stank-ass hoes Teri and Angie there," Jag said, winking.

China
Doll

"You shut your mouth. You know you love my girls. They're my only family here in Baltimore," China said, her voice getting loud. "Well, not family by blood, but you know what I mean. They're the closest thing I have to blood relations here in town."

"I know, I know," Jag said. "I was just giving you shit."

"You're good at it," China said with a giggle. "So I've been thinking," China paused, "about the wedding."

"You've had your head all wrapped up in that wedding all day, haven't you?"

"Yes but—"

"But nothin'. Let's just go to bed, I wanna do dirty things to you," Jag's voice got deep as he stood up. "Come on, baby."

"You do, do you?" China asked playfully. "Well I'm

gonna make you work for it."

"Oh, I gotta work for it? That ain't nothin' I'm not prepared to do," he said. Just then, he bent down, picked China up in his powerful arms and threw her over his shoulder.

"I'm gonna show you work" Jag said.

"No daddy, no!" China feigned childishness.

Before she knew it, China was laying on the bed and Jag was on his knees, removing her panties.

"Baby," she cooed, "do it slow."

Jag threw her panties across the room and entered her.

They made love until the sun came up, Jag spending time pleasing every erogenous zone on China's body. By the time day broke, China and Jag were glistening in the light of a sunrise, sweat-drenched from a night of unadulterated passion.

She fell asleep to Jag stroking her hair, softly whispering "I love you, baby," in her ear.

China
Doll

Chapter Three

All Fall Down

When China woke from her sleep, she didn't see Jag anywhere.

"Damn it," she thought, "I can't believe he's gone already." She exhaled deeply and looked out of her window. It was getting close to 11 o'clock and sunshine was streaming in through her red curtains. China swung her legs off the bed and planted them into her tan carpet, stretching her arms upward toward the ceiling.

"You finally awake?" Jag popped his head through the doorway, startling China.

"Jag!" she said with a jump, "I didn't realize you were still here."

"It's time for breakfast, baby," Jag said. As soon as the

word "breakfast" came out of Jag's mouth, China feared for her stomach. Jag was a lot of things – a chef he was not.

Cautiously, China left her bedroom and peered into the kitchen. Stacks of pots and pans were scattered about the kitchen and two sad plates of food sat on the dining room table. Sausage, eggs, toast, hash browns and orange juice were on the table and China sat down gingerly.

"You, you cooked," she said with an anxious look on her face.

"Hell yeah I cooked. You're not the only person around here who knows their way around the kitchen!"

"Yes I am!" China said in her head, but all she said out loud was "you're so sweet." Still, she was hesitant. She took one bite of her eggs – still raw in the middle. She felt the urge to spit them out, but when she saw the look on Jag's face, she choked them down.

"You like it, baby?"

"Yes," she said with a mouth full of raw eggs.

She poked around at the rest of her plate. "At least he didn't screw up the toast," she thought. Just then, Jag's phone rang.

"I gotta take this, baby," Jag said, with an intense look on his face. He went back into the bedroom and spoke urgently. China strained to hear but couldn't make out any words. From what she could tell of his demeanor, something was wrong.

All of the sudden, she heard him scream into the phone: "Nigga, just make it happen!" He stormed out of China's room and threw on his jacket. "I gotta go, baby."

"But we're not done with breakfast," China said, halfheartedly.

"I don't got time to waste now, China. I gotta jet." He opened the door and rushed out. China was actually relieved to see him go, considering the mess of food that was staring her in the face. She walked to the garbage can and pressed her toe down on the pedal that opened the lid.

"No. Thank you," she said, dropping the contents of her plate into the trash. She took one look at the dishes that Jag accumulated in the past few hours, pulled her yellow gloves on and got to work.

"If I mess my nails up, Jag's ass is grass," she said under her breath.

After thirty minutes of washing and drying, she sat down at the kitchen table again and stared at her telephone. She wanted to call her mother and tell her about the engagement, give her all the details about the man she was getting ready to marry. She picked up the phone twice before she got the courage to dial the number.

"It has been years, China, just do it!" she commanded herself. She slowly punched the digits before hearing a few rings.

"Hello?" Myra answered. China froze. The last time she saw her mother, she slapped China in the face and spit on her, then called her an ungrateful bitch in public. Now she wanted to invite this woman to her wedding? China opened her mouth, but no words would come out.

China
Doll

"Hello?" Myra paused to listen. "Hello? Who is this?" Myra demanded to know. "You best not be fuckin' callin' my house and not sayin' shit!" Myra exploded. "Listen, motherfucker, I ain't one to be fucked with. Don't be callin' here, ever again." China slammed the receiver down onto the phone's cradle.

Some things never do change – and Myra Doll was one of those things. China stood up and walked to the bedroom for a nap, stretching out on top of the covers.

China was startled awake by an urgent knock at the door of her apartment. She rolled over and rubbed her eyes. Whoever was behind the door wasn't trying to wait long for her to open it. She drew closer to the door without making any noise, she wanted to check the peephole before opening that door. As she inched closed to the door, she put her face close to the door, nearer and nearer to the peephole. She wasn't even breathing.

The doorknob rattled back and forth as she got nearer.

She closed her eyes and took a silent deep breath, afraid of what she'd find behind through the peephole.

When she looked out and saw Jag, she lost all of her nerves and exhaled. She was so nervous for nothing!

She swung the door open. "Jag! Thank God it's you. Why were you knockin' all crazy?" She turned around and plopped down on the couch, but Jag didn't follow her. He stood motionless in the doorway.

"Jag, what are you doing?" she asked. Jag didn't respond. He took one small step into the apartment and fell to his knees.

"Jag? What are you doing?"

All Jag did was blink a few times, and coughed. He didn't cover his mouth, and blood trickled from his lips onto the carpet.

"Are you bleeding? What is going on?" China stood up, panicked.

"I fucked up, China."

At this point, China was frantic. She flew across the living room and threw her arms around him. When she looked down, he was holding his chest. She moved his hand and saw blood had soaked through his black shirt and was gathering under him in a large pool. He was sweating through his clothes, but he was getting cold.

"Jag, I don't understand. What happened to you?" Her heart beat rapidly as her adrenaline kicked in.

"DC boys," he said weakly. He started coughing again.

"What? Who was it? What happened?" China pulled her cell from her back pocket and dialed 911.

16

China
Doll

"911, what is your emergency?" The operator asked.

"My fiancé's been shot! I need an ambulance right the fuck now." China was shouting hysterically, cradling Jag in one arm and holding her phone with the other, the front door standing wide open. She tilted her head back and let out a primal scream. "Help me," she shrieked wildly.

"What is your address, where are you?" The operator asked.

"Twenty-four hundred Oaklawn Street, at the Arbor's Development,"

"Ok, an ambulance is on its way."

China threw her phone across the room and held Jag's head in her lap, wiping the sweat away from his eyes with her palms while wiping away her own tears. "Baby, what happened?"

"I fucked up, China." His eyes started to close. China slapped him across the face.

"Don't you fuckin' close your eyes," she commanded. "Don't you fuckin' leave me."

Jag feigned a smile.

"I love you," he said, as tears began welling in his eyes. "Don't forget that."

"I know you do, that's why you have to stay with me," she cried. Gradually, the wall of strength she built was breaking down, and she couldn't stay strong any longer.

"Jag, baby, please, you can't do this." Her chest heaved as she lost her breath between gasps. She was losing control. "Please baby, stay with me. Stay with me!" His eyes began to close again.

"You can't fucking leave me! Stop!" She ran her fingers along the lines in his face, knowing that this was the last time she would touch her lover while he was still alive. "Motherfucker, I need you here," she said between tears. "Come back to me."

She started counting his breaths, feeling his chest rise and fall, each time more shallow.

"Where is the fucking ambulance?" She bellowed.

China
Doll

"China," Jag said, "I," he paused.

"You what?" China cried.

"I – I" his eyes glazed over and his body went limp.

"No! No. No, no, no, Jag!" She pounded on his chest, nothing happened.

Jag died in her arms.

When the ambulance arrived, the paramedics had to physically remove China from Jag's body.

"There's nothing we can do, miss," the paramedic paused, "Miss, what's your name miss?"

She didn't answer him. She couldn't even look at him.

"I'm sorry, there's nothing we can do. We have to leave now, and we have to take him."

Still, no response from China. One paramedic, the one with a moustache, patted her on the back before his partner took out a white sheet and placed it over top Jag's body. They collected Jag's body and placed it in the ambulance on a stretcher.

China didn't move from her place on the floor, where Jag died in her arms, until she fell asleep that night, silently.

Chapter Four

Crossroads

After watching her lover die in her arms, China was broken. One morning, Teri and Angie showed up at China's doorstep and knocked until she answered. China came to the door and squinted in the sunlight.

"What are y'all doin' here?" she asked, her voice raspy for spending so much time without speaking.

"We're comin' inside, bitch. Move." Angie pushed China aside and made her way into the dank apartment. She noticed Jag's shirt sitting on the chair beside the couch, every surface covered in take out containers and pizza boxes. The air smelled stale, like no one had opened a window in months. In actuality, they hadn't.

"Girl, this is your intervention," Teri said.

"For what?" China asked apathetically.

"You've got to get outta this damn house! Your hair is ratty, you look like you haven't changed clothes in a week, you got bags under your eyes, you have got to get out of here," Angie said, emphasizing every word so China understood how serious this was.

"I don't know, I'm just not ready," China said, defeatedly.

"Not ready? You been holed up for six months, or damn near it. You gotta get outta here, clear your head, get some fresh air. This ain't workin' girl. You're gonna die in here," Angie was urgent, and she meant business for her friend.

China looked up from the couch and took a deep breath. "I know you're right – it's just hard.

"We know it's hard, baby. That's why we're here to support you," Teri said. "Right Angie?"

"Right, so let's get you together, girl. I'm gonna clean up this fuckin' shit hole while Teri gets your raggedy ass together. And you best get outta that robe. Put on some real damn clothes," Angie said, laughing. Teri led China by the hand to the bathroom and Angie got cleaning. Two hours later, Teri had trimmed China's split ends, gave her a quick manicure and pedicure, and covered her whole body with cocoa butter.

"Girl, you're already lookin' good," Angie said, who'd just finished cleaning the majority of the apartment. "Let's have a drink. Take your mind off things."

Angie walked to the cupboard and pulled out some vodka, and grabbed some cranberry juice from the refrigerator.

"It's not much, but it'll do," she said under her breath. She mixed three drinks and poured them into martini glasses, then put them down on the coffee table.

China and Teri emerged from the bathroom, and China looked like a normal person for the first time since Jag's death.

China
Doll

"Look at my girl! You don't look like a homeless person anymore. Which, is something we need to talk about. That's what you're going to be if you don't get back to work soon. They've given you two extensions, China. You have got to get back. It'll do you good to spend some time out of the house."

"I know, I know. I just–" Angie cut her off.

"You just what? No more excuses. Today is the first day of the rest of your life. It might sound corny, but whatever. Get your shit together. Jag's been gone for six months! It is time to move on."

"I know," China said, sounding defeated.

"Well, I'm glad, 'cause personally, I'm ready to have my girl back," Teri said.

"I'm lucky to have y'all," China said, sighing.

"Shit yeah you are girl! You ain't kiddin'," Angie said, laughing. "I'm glad you're snappin' out of it."

China finished up her drink and gave her friends a hug.

"Thanks y'all, I love you. You keep me real," China admitted.

She wasn't completely ready to move on, but it was a start, at least.

China
Doll

Chapter Five

Get Your Groove Back

A few months later, China had her act together more than ever. She was back working with at-risk kids, and being as sociable as she could. One night, as she was getting ready for dinner and drinks with Teri, she had a good feeling.

"Tonight's gonna be a good night," she said to herself as she slipped into a skintight black sweater and jeans, capping off the look with knee boots and a black leather jacket. She walked into the living room where Teri was waiting.

"Damn girl, look at you, all sexy."

"Don't I know it," China said with a giggle.

Teri grabbed her keys and they walked to the car.

A few minutes later, they were at a bar down the street.

"I'm starving. I really hope we don't have to wait forever to get a table," she said as they pulled up two barstools.

"Here, eat these," China said, pushing a bowl of pretzels in Teri's direction. "You always hungry?"

"Damn straight," Teri said.

Finally seated at a table near the window, China was preoccupied by the people walking on the sidewalk outside.

"What are you getting?" Teri asked as she thumbed through the menu.

"I was thinking steak, maybe, or that chicken pasta they make here."

After giving the waiter their order, they settled into the booth and made idle conversation. Just at that moment, something caught China's eye. A man, across the bar from them, was staring in their direction.

"Oh my God, girl. Don't look now, but that nigga at the bar looks just like Jag," China whispered.

"Are you serious?" Teri looked toward the man as nonchalantly as she could.

"Damn girl, you're right. He does. You OK?" Teri asked, empathetically.

"Yeah, I know Jag's gone – that much is for sure. But, damn, he looks just like him," China said through clenched teeth.

Out of nowhere, the waiter appeared with two glasses of champagne.

"Ladies, compliments of the gentleman at the bar," the waiter said. Teri giggled.

"Damn, knowin' how to treat a lady," Teri said as she raised her glass to China. "Who was it?" Teri asked, as she looked toward the bar. The man who resembled Jag nodded in her direction, winked and smiled. China was hiding her face out of embarrassment. Teri raised her glass

24

China
Doll

to the man.

"Is he trying to impress me or you?" China asked.

"I don't even know, but we're about to find out. He's walking over here."

"He best not hit on me, I'm not even ready to handle somethin' like that," China warned. She felt someone approach from behind, but didn't look.

"Ladies," he said in a deep voice, "I wanted to introduce myself. I'm Blake."

"Well, hello Blake. I'm Teri, and this is my best friend, China. It's nice to meet you," Teri flirted.

Blake took China's hand and kissed it softly.

"It's nice to meet you, China." His grip lingered on her skin. "Are you here alone?"

"Actually yes, we are. We were just havin' a relaxing girls' night out," Teri answered. China began breathing heavily.

"Well I just met my friends here for drinks, I'll leave you to your drinks," Blake said smoothly.

"Well, if you want to join us, we wouldn't mind," Teri cooed. Blake nodded and went back to his friends. He collected another strong, muscular dark skinned man and started talking quietly.

China shot Teri attitude from across the table.

"Nigga what the fuck is you doin" China hissed.

"Bitch, don't get hood. They're cute, lets just have dinner and see what happens." Teri said with enough attitude to put her friend in her place.

China eased up and thought about the last time she actually touched a man. It had been close to a year.

Just then, Blake and his friend approached the table.

"Kurt, this is China. Teri, this is Kurt," Blake said, as he took a seat directly beside China. "Now that we're all friends, let's grub."

Everyone in the bar was staring at them. They were definitely the only thing going at the bar. Four attractive people who looked like they were on a perfect double date. The only problem was the sinking feeling China felt in the pit of her stomach.

"Excuse me," she said. "I need to use the ladies room. Teri?"

"No, I don't gotta go. You'll be fine, girl," she said, looking back into Kurt's eyes. They were vibing, hard.

China headed toward the ladies room, but just as she was about to open the door, she heard someone approach from behind her. She twirled around to see which sad sack had followed her, but Blake stood right in front of her.

"Oh, hi. Sorry. I didn't realize that was you."

"It's ok, baby. I just wanted to give you this," he said, and handed her a small piece of paper. She unfolded it and saw Blake's name with a phone number scribbled alongside it.

"I didn't wanna get shut down in front of my boy, so I thought I'd let you shut me down here. Save my pride," he said, smiling. China respected the swagger, but still wasn't convinced.

"What makes you think you're gonna get shut down?"

"Not sure, just a feeling. You've been pretty quiet" he said. China didn't let him in on the fact it was because he was a dead ringer for her deceased fiancé.

"Well, maybe I will, maybe I won't," China said, trying to flirt but failing miserably.

"It only takes a phone call, Ma," Blake said in the sexiest voice he could muster. China turned around, used the restroom and returned to the table where Teri looked like she'd give her right arm to sleep with Kurt – he had her open.

"Well, Teri, looks like it's about time to go. We've been here almost four hours," China said. "I need to get home before I drink too much."

"Can you tell she's the responsible one?" she said to the men. "I gotta work early too, let's get outta here."
Kurt looked like a disappointed puppy, he thought he was

getting' some tonight.

On the way to the car, China heard a voice behind her call her name.

"China!" She turned to see who was calling her. It was Blake.

"Yeah," she answered. "You sure know how to sneak up behind a girl, don't you?"

"Naw, I just wanted to make sure you still had that number," he said. Teri's eyes got wide and she nodded, then got into the passenger seat in the car.

"Yeah, I got it."

"Well, you wanna give me a call when you're home? I wanna make sure you get back OK."

"Oh, you wanna check up on it already?" China said with a toss of her hair. Her game was coming back little by little.

"If you're lucky," she whispered, and got into her car.

She never called him when she got home. She wanted to make him wait.

27

China
Doll

Chapter Six

Going Downtown

"It's Saturday night! Let's hit the town bitches!" Teri hollered as her and Angie ran into China's apartment.

"Where are we going tonight?" China asked.

"Club Fire, downtown. It opens tonight, no way it can't be hot," Angie said.

The three girls got ready, each wearing something more sexy than the next. By the time they got to the club, it was almost midnight and the whole place was packed.

As soon as they got in, Teri headed to the bar. "Y'all want anything?" Teri asked.

China handed her a $50 bill, "Yeah, grab me a vodka cranberry and whatever y'all want. This round's on me."

Angie bobbed her head to the beat, "Tequila Sunrise,

baby."

While Teri got the drinks, China and Angie headed to the VIP. As Teri approached, she was wearing a grin from ear to ear.

"Guess who's here?"

"Who?" China asked, secretly hoping it was Blake and his friends.

"You know it, girl," Teri said, raising a glass to her friends.

"Did you talk to them?" China asked.

"Kurt came over first," she paused, "so I invited them up here."

"Oh, so I'm just supposed to sit here like a fifth wheel while y'all laugh it up with these niggas?" Angie said, rolling her head.

"Hell no, girl. They got a friend for you. You met Kurt?" Teri asked her.

China
Doll

"No, but is he the nigga in the black cap with the braids?," Angie trailed off.

"That's him."

"Mm, girl, I can't even be mad at ya," she said. They locked arms and sauntered toward the men, like jaguars approaching their prey.

China tossed back her drink and felt the vodka rush down her throat. She was nervous, but she knew that she had to keep her game tight. Out of the corner of her eye, she spotted Blake headed straight toward her. His eyes were fixed on her, and she couldn't help but feel a little awkward. She stood up and met him halfway.

"It's good to see you," China said.

"It's been too long. I thought you were gonna call me." Blake said bluntly.

"I got busy."

"I see, well, you look amazing tonight, baby," Blake gave China elevator eyes.

"I know," she said with a smirk. "Let's go sit. I just wanted to say hello before we got over there."

"Well hello to you too, Ma."

They rejoined their friends and Blake ordered two bottles of Moët. When the waitress left, he put his hand on China's thigh.

"Excuse me?" she said. He immediately took his hand off her leg. China reached for her glass, but it was empty. Blake noticed and grabbed her hand.

"Come on, let me buy you another," he said. Blake led China by the hand, but didn't stop at the bar. He walked right past it and kept walking into a darkened hallway.

"Where are we going?" China asked, "Where are you taking me?"

"You'll see," Blake said with a grin, and opened a door at the end of a long, empty hallway. He pulled her inside and turned around and held her tight.

"I just wanted you to myself for a minute," he said.

China looked around the dark room and couldn't see much. A desk, a few chairs and a lamp were the only things visible in the dim light. She couldn't even speak as Blake wrapped his arms around her waist, kissing her tenderly on the forehead. He pulled her toward him and lifted her chin toward his full lips.

China Doll

"I've been wanting to get close to you since I first saw you," Blake said, looking down at China. He stood over six inches taller than her, and China was wearing four-inch stilettos.

In one motion, Blake lifted China up, pinned her against the wall and pulled her panties to the side. China didn't make a sound. It had been too long since she was with a man, and her body was screaming for Blake, lust was winning over reason.

"Wait," China said, feeling the urge to stop, but unwilling to walk away. Blake took one finger and put it to her lips.

"Shh," he whispered, unbuckling his belt with his free hand. Before China could say no, he was putting himself inside her.

"Blake," she whispered. Her body started shaking from the pleasure, and the feeling that they might be caught at any moment only made it more intense.

"Oh baby, fuck me," China said. She sounded hungry for it. Her breathing got faster and more shallow, and his steady strokes got stronger and stronger. The muscles in China's stomach knotted and within minutes, China was sweating and calling Blake's name. "Blake! Fuck me!" China screamed. "Oh my God, I'm gonna come."

"Baby, I'm there," Blake said. "I'm so close," he moaned into her neck. His breathing got heavy. "You feel so fuckin' good." He continued his rhythm, lifting China up and sitting her on top of him.

"Baby, oh my God," she moaned, losing control. Their bodies were in sync, moving up and down, faster and harder.

"I'm gonna come," China growled, nearly there.

China Doll

"Me too," Blake said, and at that moment, they came at the same time, slowing down gradually while they stared into each other's eyes. China collapsed onto Blake, still silently grinding into him.

"Damn girl," Blake said, wiping sweat from his brow.

"That was on point, B," China said as she took a deep breath, trying to collect herself. She smoothed her hair, and put her skirt and panties back into place.

"Blake," China started to feel awkward and whorish.

"What's wrong, baby?" He asked.

"For the record, I ain't a ho," China said bluntly, feeling a bit embarrassed by what she just did.

"Look, we're both grown-ass people, no regrets," he said. China nodded her head, but didn't look fully convinced. "Go back to the table, and I'll grab drinks and meet you there," he said, stuffing his impressive member back into his pants.

"Ok," China said softly, walking away with a knitted brow. When China got back to the table, it was completely empty, except for a few empty bottles. She turned around to see Kurt and Tommy dancing with Teri and Angie, who both were both working it on the dance floor.

Blake returned to the table and sat down next to China, and then handed her the vodka cranberry. She tossed her head back, and in one hurried gulp, finished it. It didn't seem to calm her nerves much, because when Blake threw his arm around her, she recoiled away from him.

Blake put his lips close to China's ear so she could hear him over the bumpin' music.

"Don't be trippin'. Listen. I go after what I want, and I live in the moment. I haven't gotten you off my mind since the first time I saw you."

China looked around nervously for something else to calm her nerves. She picked up Blake's shot of Hennessey and tossed it back. The DJ was on the last song of the night, and all China was thinking about was getting away from Blake.

"This went too fast," she thought. "I have got to go."

Soon, the lights came up and everyone started heading to the lot to find their cars. Blake led China by the hand from the booth to find her girlfriends. Once they were outside, Blake leaned against her car and reached for her, laying her head on his chest.

"Hey girl, you ready?" Teri and Angie hollered from the other side of the lot. China nodded her head.

"Yeah, it's gettin' late," China said, half drunk. Blake handed her another one of his cards.

"Use it this time," he told her. "See you ladies later," Blake said, walking toward Kurt and Tommy.

As soon as the girls were in the car, the questions started.

"Don't even be thinkin' about turnin' that stereo on, girl. Where'd you and Blake dip off to?" Teri asked.

"What are you talking about?" China said, half-heartedly.

"Shit, bitch. Just 'fess the fuck up."

33

China Doll

There wasn't any sense in denying anything or lying right to Teri and Angie's faces.

"Not pay attention, 'cause I ain't about to repeat this," China said before recounting the story in every lurid detail.

"Well, was it good?" Teri asked.

"It had to be. My girl let it go down, so there ain't no doubt!" Angie said.

"That nigga had you open, China! It's good though. Kurt wants to hang tomorrow, and if you're already giving up the poon poon, I don't think I'll have anything to be worried about," she said, laughing hard.

China forced a laugh and blasted the radio for the rest of the ride home. Although she knew she didn't do anything wrong, per say. They were both adults who wanted each other – but she still felt like she had something to feel guilty about.

Angie and Teri walked China up to the door of her apartment and made sure she locked herself in. China staggered toward the bedroom and stripped down to her bra and panties before diving face-first into bed. The softness of her blankets made her feel sleepy, but she could still smell Blake all over her. She reached toward her phone and took another breath in before dialing.

"Yo," Blake answered.

"Hey, it's China."

"What's up, you home?"

"Yeah. I wanted to ask you somethin'." Blake cleared his throat.

"Yeah, what's goin' on?" he asked.

"What made you think you could come at me like that. I had no idea that tonight was gonna go down like it did."

Blake laughed. "Listen, like I said earlier – I live in the moment, and I go after what I want." He spoke frankly.

"So how did you know what was back there?" China asked.

"I've done business back in the backroom once or

twice. There's never anyone back there." He didn't let her get a word in edgewise. "You're not getting it though. I don't fuck with any bitch. Most bitches ain't worth shit. I'm not runnin' shit like that. I need a bitch with her shit together."

China could tell game from a mile away, and this was right in front of her face.

"Hmm," China said. She wasn't convinced, but still wanted to see him again.

"Well, since you ain't trustin' me, let's chill tomorrow night," he sighed. "I'm fuckin' beat – but if you wanna find out what kinda man I am, we can make it happen."

"We might be able to work somethin' out," China said, hesitantly.

"Well, I'll call you tomorrow. If you answer, it's on. If you don't, then I hear you loud and clear. Where you live?" he asked.

"The arbors," China said with little emotion.

"Expect my call around nine," he said. "Peace."

China wasn't convinced she'd see him again. She didn't even know if he'd call her the next day, but she stretched out her arms and smiled, stomach filled with butterflies.

35

China Doll

Chapter Seven

Black and Blue

China's phone rang, and she waited four rings before she answered it. She didn't want to look too eager. When she picked it up and looked at the caller ID, she was disappointed when it read "Angie."

"Hey China, you coming out with us tonight? We're 'bout to get it poppin'," she said with a grunt.

"No, I'm supposed to hang with Blake."

Angie took a moment and hit her cigarette, blowing the smoke from the side of her mouth.

"Really. What are you supposed to do?"

"Shit if I know, girl. I wanna see what this nigga's all about. I don't even know what to think of him."

"Alright, well if somethin' falls through, we'll be at

the club. Same one as last night."

"Girl, you 'bout to hit the same club twice in a weekend?"

"Ain't nothin' else goin' down tonight. Tommy and Kurt are goin', so we figured 'why the fuck not?'"

"Shit, girl. No way I'm gettin' into anything like that. Have fun though, holler at ya girl."

"Bye bitch," Angie said with a smile before hanging up.

As soon as China put her phone down, she picked it back up without looking at the caller ID.

"Bitch, you miss me already? What's up, you wanna borrow shoes or what?"

A man's voice echoed through the ear piece.

"I'm not really that kind of guy," Blake said.

China froze.

*China
Doll*

"Shit! I'm sorry," he caught her off guard. "I thought you were someone else."

"Apparently you did. So, you got plans tonight?" Of course she didn't. She'd been waiting on his call all afternoon.

"A few things are happenin', but I don't know. I'm thinkin' of just layin' in the cut," she lied.

"Well, I'm on my way over. I'm about fifteen out."

"Fifteen? Shit, nigga. You best give me more time than that. I gotta get ready."

"Alright baby, you got thirty. Get to steppin'," he said with a smile.

"See you when you get here. I'm apartment C, first floor.

"Well that's easy enough to remember. See you soon, baby."

China rushed around the house getting ready, but tried to not look too put-together. She heard a knock on the door right on time.

"Well hello," he said, looking China up and down.

"What's up?" China asked as nonchalantly as possible,

walking into her apartment and plopping down on a recliner.

"Not a damn thing," he said, closing and locking the door behind him. He walked over to the couch and sat down. He looked to his left and saw a photo of a man.

"Who's this?" Blake asked.

"That's my father."

"You got his nose," he said.

"That's what my mother told me," China said.

"If she looks anything like you, I bet Momma looks good," Blake said slyly.

"We don't talk." China crossed her arms.

"Oh, hit a nerve?" Blake asked.

"Hit a nerve? I don't know, the woman just beat the shit out of me for my entire childhood for no reason whatsoever until I left for college and cut her out of my life. Sure, you might've hit a nerve."

"Whoa, girl." Blake looked surprised at her honesty. "Didn't mean to get into anything deep."

"I'm sorry," China sighed. "I got a lot of hate for that woman."

"You must," Blake answered. "Well, if it makes you feel any better, shit with my mom ain't any better, but she ain't never laid a finger on me. Just left one day and never looked back."

They both sat in silence and stared at the ground.

"Shit. I didn't mean to take it there. I don't even know you and here I am spilling family secrets," China said. "Unnecessary." She got up and grabbed a bottle of Hennessey from the cupboard.

"You want?" she asked.

"I do," Blake answered.

After a few drinks, they were a bit more loosened up – avoiding depressing topics of conversation.

After three hours of drinking together, they were sitting on the same couch, China with her legs folded underneath her, Blake sprawled back on the couch.

39

China
Doll

"So, what's your deal, China?" Blake asked.

"What's my deal? What do you mean what's my deal?"

"I mean you have a job, a car, your own place. You don't seem like a crackhead or a chickenhead. What's up, you crazy?"

China shook her head and laughed.

"Aren't we all?" She smiled.

"No, seriously. You seem like a 'no games' kinda bitch."

"That's something I take pride in. No games, no bullshit. I'm for real, all day."

"That must've been what I saw in you. I just can't get you outta my head. It's crazy, you'll be runnin' around my mind all day, all long."

China wanted to admit the same thing, but didn't want to tip her hand. She hadn't had as much Hennessey as Blake.

"Well, I'm a down-ass bitch," China laughed.

"Maybe it's the drink talkin', but I feel like I wanna get to know you better," Blake said. He even sounded Sincere. "But you gotta make sure this is some 'no games' shit."

It sounded perfect in theory.

"No games." China said bluntly.

"So we trust each other?"

"I ain't got a reason not to," China responded.

They talked for a while longer. After a few laughs and a bit more serious discussion, China felt like there was something in Blake that was worth getting to know more.

From that night on, they were fairly serious about each other. From what China knew, Blake wasn't out chasing tail, and after a few weeks, she lost interest in other men. He held it down in the bedroom and handled his business every night. He also spoiled China in every way. He draped her in furs, diamonds and gold, and took her to the finest restaurants in Baltimore. She never wanted for everything

– but all of this came with a price tag. Blake had serious control issues.

From the time they decided to be exclusive, Blake made it well known that he was the man and he'd sets the rules – and there were rules for everything. There were rules as to what China could wear, when she could eat, sleep, what she did during the day and what she'd feed him at night. That was her primary job, first off. She was responsible for feeding and fucking him, and she was to look sexy while doing it all.

Her friends started noticing when she fell off, not returning their phone calls and ignoring them altogether. Blake even convinced China to quit her job.

"Why you wanna work? You know I give you everything you need," he said. China believed him.

Blake would show up at China's apartment day or night, and while living the lifestyle of a spoiled wifey was nice for a while, but Blake's restrictions were starting to wear on China.

One night, as China slaved over smothered pork chops in a wife beater and thong, she called Angie to talk.

"Girl where the fuck you been? Blake got you locked up in a cell somewhere?"

"Aw, shut the fuck up, bitch. How are you? I miss your crazy ass."

"I know girl, I miss you too. What you doin'?"

"Right now? Shit, cookin' for my man."

"Cookin'? Weak. Let's go out, let's go get crazy, girl."

China sighed. She knew Blake would never let her go out without him.

"Nah, I can't. Blake will be home soon."

"You don't even know where that nigga is!" Angie moaned.

"He's handlin' business. I can't be mad at it." Just then, China heard the front door open. "He's here, Ang. Gotta go." She hung the phone up without saying goodbye and called out to Blake.

"Baby! You're home just in time. I just got dinner done," she said, plating up some cornbread, beans and pork.

"Where you at, girl?" Blake yelled.

"Kitchen, baby. Cookin' your dinner," she said, rolling her eyes.

He walked into the kitchen and squared off with her.

"What's wrong, baby?" she asked. He handed her an unmarked white envelope.

"What is it?" she asked. Her hands trembled a little, she didn't know what was going on.

"Just open it." he said with no emotion whatsoever. He almost sounded angry.

She took the envelope and looked at it. No markings, no clue to what it could be. She turned it over and slipped one finger into the slit, opening the envelope slowly, like there could be something dangerous inside. The first thing she saw was a barcode. She turned the contents over to read the front.

China Doll

"One way, first class. Baltimore to Jamaica," it said on the first line. "American Airlines, flight #4456."

Her eyes widened. "Blake!" She looked at him in disbelief. "Jamaica? When?"

"Tomorrow night. I gotta get outta town till the weather breaks."

"Till the weather breaks? That's over a month."

"Let's go get dinner. Let's celebrate."

"Baby, I just cooked dinner, I made your favorite."

Blake ignored her and got in the shower. "Come here," he yelled.

China stepped into the bathroom and called in to him, "yeah?"

"Get in here."

China took her wife beater and thong off and stepped into the shower. Blake started rubbing soap all over her body and started massaging her nipples. He pushed her against the shower wall and put two fingers inside of her.

"Yeah baby, that's what I like," China said. "Fuck me, Blake. Oh my God, more. Fuck me baby."

Blake's dick was hard, but instead of putting it in China's sweet spot, he turned her around and slid his throbbing penis it into her ass.

"Baby, no," China gasped. She tried to push him off of her but it was too late. She squirmed and tried to get away, but the more she tried, the more he tightened his grip.

"Baby, please, take it out," China winced in pain.

"Don't talk when I'm fuckin' you," Blake said. When he finished, he released her and turned away, allowing the water to run off of his body. When he was clean, he left the shower to get ready. "Let's go, China. Don't be takin' all night.

Defeated, she cleaned her ass and stepped out of the shower with tears in her eyes.

"Hurry the fuck up, China. I'm hungry."

"I'm not going," China said in defiance.

"The hell you're not," he responded. With those words, China felt a rush of adrenaline and jumped in Blake's face like a raging bull.

"I said I'm not fucking going!" she screamed. She was using every ounce of strength she had, chest heaving in anxiety. Blake stood unfazed. He took one step back and wound up, slapping China across the room.

"Bitch, you know better than to get up in my grill. Shut the fuck up and get the fuck ready. I'm not gon' tell you again," he threatened coldly.

China had a red handprint across her face and her eyes filled with tears, though she was too scared to cry.

"Don't you ever get in my fuckin' face again," he uttered. His eyes were dark and empty, much like her mother's used to look after she beat China when she was young. She knew that look all too well.

China dressed in silence, her face stinging, without any apology from the lips of her so-called lover. He

43

China
Doll

showed no signs of remorse. Then, they drove silently to the restaurant where Kurt, Tommy, Teri and Angie were waiting. China shut her eyes tight when she realized her best friends would be there – and they would probably ask why her face was starting to bruise in the shape of Blake's hand. She sleeked her hair down against her face, trying to hide what she could. She decided that she would fake it through the rest of the night – masquerading as a happy, loved woman. On the inside, she just wanted to throw up.

After dinner, Blake ordered more champagne and China excused herself to use the bathroom.

"I need to use the ladies' room," she said quietly. Blake grabbed her by the arm and gave her a jerk.

"Get your shit together," he said through clenched teeth. She nodded and forced a smile, walking toward the bathroom.

"Just make it through tonight. No one will know. Just make it through this one night," China told herself. "We're leaving for Jamaica tomorrow. It can't get any worse, can it?"

She cried one tear in the bathroom and walked back to the table.

China
Doll

Chapter Eight

Vacation

The very next morning, Blake and China left for their trip to the Caribbean. The first thing China did was send a text message to Angie letting her know they were staying in Montego Bay, just in case she ended up "missing."

As soon as China stepped off the plane, she was ecstatic.

"Blake, I've never been anywhere but Atlanta and Baltimore. This is amazing. Within an hour they were standing on white sandy beaches. "Look around, Blake! We're in paradise!" Blake didn't seem impressed. Actually, he seemed a bit depressed.

China spent the next week sitting in a lounge chair, sipping tropical drinks and taking in the sunshine. Oddly,

Blake spent most of his days in the room, watching satellite television.

"Blake, you didn't come all the way to Jamaica to watch television, did you?"

"I'm just tired, baby. I just want to relax on my vacation, OK?" China didn't respond – she just nodded and walked out to the deck for a dip in resort's pool. After a swim and a snack, China returned to the room to check on Blake.

"Baby, let's get ready for dinner. C'mon, let's go stuff ourselves crazy." Blake didn't respond, he just pulled the covers over his head.

"Go get your nails done or something. Get a massage."

"Baby! Before you know it, we'll be gone. Come on. Let's go do something."

Blake turned over, his eyes bloodshot.

"I'm just tired."

"Baby, what's wrong?" China asked, concerned. She sat down right beside him.

"I just can't do this anymore," he said with tears in his eyes. "I'm tired of this shit. Everybody wants something from me, everyone wants a piece of me."

China stroked his forehead.

"Who are you talking about?" she asked, concerned.

"You, my boys, everybody. I can't keep nobody happy."

China seized this opportunity to break her feelings down.

"Baby, you know I'm here for you. I don't care about none of that shit: the money, the clothes, none of that. I just want you to treat me right. You don't gotta do nothin' but treat me right," she said, sincerely.

He laughed.

"It don't matter, huh? You'd just fuck with any ol' regular nigga? I know you're lyin'. You just want me cause I keep you in fine ass clothes, we go to good ass restaurants and I got that money."

"No, no, no. That's not true. I just love you, Blake. She grabbed hid face with both hands and looked at Blake straight in the eyes.

"All that matters is us – me and you. Together. That's it. I mean that."

Immediately, he laid China on the bed and made love to her. He was attentive to every part of her body and poured himself into pleasuring her in every way he knew how.

"Oh baby, you feel so good." He ran his fingers through her hair and kissed her deeply. "China, China" he murmered over and over again.

The next three weeks in Jamaica were the most romantic weeks the two of them had ever seen in their entire lives. Most of the time they had left was spent making love, feeding each other and talking about the new lives they wanted to start together. China's face was red from smiling so much – a real happiness that laughed in the face of her mother's abuse.

China Doll

Finally, after five weeks of paradise, it was time to leave and return home. On the flight back, Blake seemed more in love with China than he ever had. He held her hand and his eyes welled with tears. Out of the blue, he started talking about his past.

"When I was younger, my mom used to run through men like it was her job. Every time she had one that was serious enough to bring into the house, she'd automatically start calling him 'my new daddy.' For the most part, I could deal because they didn't fuck with me and I didn't fuck with them."

China just watched Blake attentively and listened. He was noticeably uncomfortable.

"Then she brought home this dude Havoc. Well, his name was Percy, but all the niggas in the neighborhood called him Havoc 'cause he'd kill somebody over a dime. Come up short on Havoc and you'd end up beaten to death in a dumpster."

Little by little, Blake stopped resembling the man who made love to China in Jamaica, and they weren't even back on the ground yet.

"When he moved in, I knew shit was gonna get rough. One night while mom was working, he came in drunk as shit. He called for me, and I got out of bed and went downstairs. Mind you, this was like two, three o'clock in the morning." He stopped and took a drink of his ginger ale. "He told me to clean the house up or he'd have my ass. After he passed out on the couch, I got to cleaning. Halfway through the kitchen, I ended up falling asleep on the kitchen table."

"How old were you when this happened?"

"Eight years old. So, like I was sayin', I was asleep, and when I woke up he was standing right behind me. He was pissed, screamin' and hollerin', and all I could do was cry. When he took his belt off, I thought I was gonna get whooped. I was surprised when he dropped his pants to the floor."

China's eyes widened and she grabbed Blake's hand. She held her breath, hoping she wouldn't hear what was coming next.

"I never seen a dick so big in my life. He grabbed me from the chair and bent me over the kitchen table, tellin' me he'd give me something to cry about. I screamed and screamed 'til I lost my voice, and nothin'. That nigga tore my shit open, then, just to top it off, when he was done, he beat me unconscious."

"Oh my God," China said, wiping away tears of sympathy."

"When I woke up, I was in the hospital with a broken arm, a battered body and a stitched-up ass. The old bitty next door found me the next morning. My mom never came for me. A few weeks later I found out she skipped town with Havoc. I ain't seen her since," he said.

"Where'd you go after that? Who took care of you?"

China
Doll

China asked.

"Well, the old lady who found me gave me a bed for a while, and when she died I went to my grandmother's who didn't really want me. She used to beat the living shit out of me too."

"Jesus, Blake. I had no idea," China said, stroking his face.'

"Not something I talk about that often," Blake said, before getting silent for the rest of ride home.

When China and Blake got home, the bliss they experienced in Jamaica was all but gone. Blake went back to the game, and China went back to being a prisoner in her own home. It was time for a real change, China thought. It was time for her to make moves.

49

China
Doll

Chapter Nine

Back to Square One

More than anything, Jamaica woke China back up, made her hungry again. She knew to keep this momentum going, she would have to get back to work. Her head was filled with memories of the at-risk kids she would mentor, guiding the kids in a positive way, in a world where positivity was hard to find.

She still didn't know how to address the subject with Blake. She waited up late for him one night, and when he got home, he seemed more agitated than normal. What's the worst that could happen, she thought, he'll just say no?

"Baby, what are you doing awake? It's four o'clock in the morning," Blake sneered.

"I thought I'd wait up for you tonight, see my baby," China said.

"What do you want, China? I'm tired. I'm not in the mood for any bullshit."

China cut to the chase. "I waited up for you because I want to tell you that I need to go back to work. I can't just stay cooped up in this apartment all day and night. I never see my friends, I don't have any family, all I have is you, and you're here to sleep and eat. I need something for myself, too." China took a sigh of relief, so far, so good.

"Turn off that light," Blake said, and rolled over on the bed."

"Seriously, Blake. I can start taking over part of the bills, because my boss called today and said I could have my job back if I wanted it. They're really shorthanded and need someone there as soon as possible."

Blake sat up and gave China a dirty look.

China
Doll

"What did I say?" he spat. "I been in the streets all day and I gotta come home to your shit? I can't get no peace nowhere, can I?"

"Baby I'm not trying to argue, I'm just trying to do something for myself, something for us."

"Something for us? How about you shut the fuck up and let me sleep? That's something you could do for us."

"Blake, I don't understand. I'm just trying to give something to this relationship. You work so hard and I just sit here all day. I just want to take some pressure off of you."

Blake sat up in bed and jumped up, pulling China out of bed by the ankles.

"Bitch don't you listen? I told you to shut the fuck up! You're not happy? Is that what you're trying to say?" Blake took China by the face and pounded it against the mirror. "Take a look at your damn self, China. Platinum, furs, expensive trips and endless money, I gave you all that shit! Now look at you! You didn't have none of that shit till I got here. I never forced you to take none of this shit!"

China slipped out of his grip and darted across the room.

"You think you can put your fuckin' hands on me, nigga? You best check yourself," China screamed, head rolling from side to side.

Blake started walking toward her, so China picked up a snowglobe from the dresser and threw it at him, grazing his ear. Blake stopped, surprised China would put up a fight, and put his hand to his ear. When he rubbed his ear and looked at his fingers, he saw a small trickle of blood.

"Bitch, you done fucked up," he said with a clenched jaw.

China didn't even see it coming. Blake grabbed her by the hair and threw her to the floor, then he hocked up a ball of phlegm from his throat and spit in her face.

"You think you can fuckin' throw shit at me? Nobody puts their fuckin' hands on me, bitch! What'd I tell you?" His voice was booming. "All I wanted to do was fuckin' sleep and you had to keep running your fuckin' mouth. That's your problem, China. You don't know when to shut the fuck up," he said, head bobbing from left to right.

Blake came down on her again, like a crackhead who cheated him out of $10, he was fighting to inflict pain – nothing else. He was all over her, and when he tired, he put his shirt back on and left the apartment with the front door wide open.

When China regained consciousness, she crawled into the bathroom and pulled herself up to the mirror to see what had happened. She didn't know how much time had passed, but she was alone, her eye was swollen shut, blood poured down from a gash in her forehead. She struggled to stand, but couldn't muster the strength to stand up. She made her way back to her bed and floated in and out of consciousness until finally succumbing to sleep.

"Teri! Call 911!" Angie screamed.

Teri dialed as soon as she could pull her cell from her

purse.

"The Arbors. Apartment C, first floor. Female. Yes, hurry please!"

"Can you hear me, China?" someone asked

"Please just leave me alone, I just want to sleep."

"China, if you can hear me, open your eyes," the voice demanded. China moaned, and a gurgle came from her stomach.

The last thing China saw was a paramedic, dressed in blue, strapping her onto something. After that, it was back to black.

China spent the next two weeks in the hospital recovering from three broken rubs, internal bleeding, a fractured skill, several contusions and many stitches. Teri and Angie took turns staying at her bedside so she wasn't alone. China did not wake up for the first three days. When she did wake up, she was incoherent from all of the pain medication, but she knew full well how she got there.

When Angie took China home from the hospital, she walked into her apartment and stopped dead in her tracks at the giant bloodstain on the hallway carpet. When I asked around, no one had heard from Blake, but she knew the cycle of abuse too well by now. He couldn't be too far away.

"You've gotta stay with me, Angie," China said, looking at her friend with sad eyes. "I can't be here by myself."

Angie nodded and gave China a soft kiss on the cheek. In twenty minutes, Teri had arrived Chinese take-out and a stack of DVDs. They sat in the living room together and watching cheesy romantic comedies until China fell asleep. That night, around ten o'clock, they heard a loud pounding at the door. Teri and Angie sat straight up.

China Doll

"If that motherfucker is on the other side of that door, I'm gonna kill him," Teri said.

"His black ass better get to steppin'," Angie agreed.

All of the sudden, the knob turned. Blake was keying in to the apartment. Teri grabbed a baseball bat and Angie grabbed a lamp and pulled the cord out of the wall. Blake walked in, slowly.

"Whoa, whoa, whoa. I'm not here to fight," he said, hands raised.

"Oh, this time, you're not tryin' to fight. Sorry ass nigga."

"I just want to talk to China. That's all. I just want to talk."

"You have five minutes," China said. "Ladies, go to my room. Come back in five minutes."

"No! Fuck this China! I'm calling the cops!" Angie said.

"Angie," China said, with daggers in her eyes. "Shut up and do what I say. Go to my room and come back in five minutes. Both of you."

China looked up at Blake.

"Talk."

"Well, I just wanted to come here to say I'm sorry. I've been thinking a lot about," China cut him off.

"You've been thinking? You've been thinking Blake? I have three broken ribs, and one of my fucking eyes is swollen shut. What have you been thinking about, exactly?"

Blake looked at her blankly. "I just wanted to take care of you. I know what I did was wrong, and I've been beating myself up for it each and every day. I can't make excuses for it, but I know shit got out of hand," he said.

"Out of hand? Shit got out of hand? Nigga you put me in the hospital! Get the fuck outta my house," China screamed frantically.

Blake sat down next to her. "Baby, just hear me out. I'm sorry. I really am. I love you, you know that. Remember

55

China Doll

Jamaica? Remember how cool we were? I want that again, I want you back." He leaned in for a kiss.

"Blake," China said calmly, "we have been through a lot. We both know that. So, all I can say now is one thing," China leaned in closer and caressed the side of Blake's face tenderly. "Get your black ass out of my motherfucking house before I call the cops on your triflin' ass."

Blake looked into China's eyes and gasped.

"Did you hear me or did I stutter? Get the fuck out!"

Teri and Angie ran into the room.

"China, don't do this to me, you can't. You can't do this to me."

"Can you not hear? She said to get the fuck out this house!" Angie screamed.

"Get the fuck out, nigga. Get yo' black ass outta this house," she flicked her wrists and pointed toward the door. Blake hung his head and walked out of the apartment. As soon as he left the threshold, Angie slammed the door behind him.

"I can't believe that piece of shit. Good fuckin' riddance," Teri yelled.

China didn't look as happy as both of her friends.

"I'm back at square fuckin' one," she said. How many times can a person be pushed back to the starting point of their life? No matter how many times I make steps toward gettin' somewhere, I get dragged right back to where I started. My father, my mother and now this!"

"You'll be OK, baby," Teri said, rubbing China's shoulders.

"You gotta know you're better off without his crazy ass," Angie added, wiping the tears from China's face.

Teri paced the floor, angry as hell. "You should've let me take a bat to that nigga! Coming in here like everything is cool. Can you believe him? I can't stand him." She was fuming with anger.

China didn't have much to say. She sank in her bed and cried a few tears while Angie and Teri got rid of all of the remnants of Blake.

China
Doll

Chapter Ten

Control Issues

The very next day, China called and had new locks on the door and had a security system installed – whatever it would take to keep her safe. For weeks, everywhere she went, she looked over her shoulder, afraid she would run into Blake. He hadn't called or made attempts to see her, so her fears were beginning to subside, although never fully. The cycle of abuse had been on repeat with China for years, so she was finally feeling like she had some room to breathe. She started again at her job, and focusing on the kids' problems, problems she herself faced daily, was somewhat cathartic for her. Helping those children, in a way, made her feel better about her own situation. In an odd way, it was a little like therapy.

China's coworkers made her life better too. Steve, who China had known since her initial move to Baltimore years ago, made work fun and gave China a sense of comfort and continuity.

At six-feet-one, Steve's chiseled body matched well with his easy, pleasant personality. He was a good-looking guy in his early thirties, a few years older than China. Steve was also gay as the day is long, and he was proud of it. He wasn't the flamboyant type, but he also had no problem talking about it with anyone who asked. China liked talking to Steve, mostly because she got a man's point of view on her life, without any of the sexual tension. She trusted him almost as much as Teri and Angie.

"Let's go get a drink," Steve suggested one day after work. "It's been a long week."

"Ok," China responded. "You're right. This week's been a bitch."

China
Doll

They walked to the bar down the street from where they worked, a low-key bar and grille where they sat at a small circular table and ordered a round right away.

"I'm glad you asked me out, Steve, we need more time like this. I hate just seeing you at work," China said.

"I've been tryin' to get you out for weeks," Steve said with a smile. "It's good to know you don't turn into a pumpkin right after work. I was starting to wonder if you were real or not." They both laughed.

"Damn it feels good to laugh again," China said.

"What do you mean?" Steve asked.

"It's just been a really crazy month."

"Man problems?" Steve said through cut eyes.

"You have no idea."

"Well tell me about it," Steve said, focusing all of his attention on China.

Over the next four rounds of drinks, China recounted the good, the bad and the ugly of her time with Blake. The more she told, the wider Steve's eyes got. Most of the things she said, Steve couldn't even believe.

"You're kidding me. You let him do all this and never went to the cops?"

"If I did, it would only get worse."

"I really can't believe you, China. Imagine one of your kids came to you at work and told them that they were getting beat by their parents? What would you tell them?"

"I probably would tell them that they didn't do anything to deserve it and it's not their fault." China said, her eyes falling. "It's the fault of the abusive bastard who's hitting them. Then I would call Child Protective Services."

"Exactly. The only difference is, you don't have Protective Services. You have the police. That's how you make sure it never happens again," Steve said, getting visibly angry.

"I know, it's just," China paused.

"It's just what?"

"It's just not that easy. Blake's in the game. He's got friends. Friends who would do whatever it took," she trailed off.

"China, I can't believe you have this attitude. But," he said, cradling China's chin in his hand, "You have my support any time you need it. You just call me and I'll be there."

"Thanks, Steve," China said, wiping a tear from her eye. "Ugh! I'm so tired of crying over this guy. No more tears!"

"Exactly. Just like Mary J. says: 'No More Drama,'" Steve said, chuckling.

China laughed again.

"Well I think it's time for us to get out of here, Steve," China said. "We've got an early morning tomorrow."

"You're right," Steve said.

They gathered their things and headed for their cars. As they left the bar, she heard someone hollering at her.

"Hey Ma!" The voice said, "let me holler at you."

She turned around and saw Blake leaning against the

building next door.

"Steve, you need to go," China said.

"The hell I do," he spat back.

"China, China, China. Didn't take you long to find another nigga to fuck wit'," Blake said in disgust.

"You got the wrong idea, bud," Steve said.

"Oh, do I?" Blake responded, looking at Steve up and down. "He don't look like your type, China. He's too pretty."

"He's gay, Blake. We work together. We're just friends."

"Gay? Nigga don't look gay. You gay nigga?" Blake asked with squinted eyes.

Steve stuck his chest out and threw his shoulders back. He could easily intimidate most men, mostly because his arms were like tree trunks.

"Yeah. I fuck men. I also ain't scared to fuck men up." He looked straight at Blake.

"Steve, stop it! I ain't havin' this, no way," China said. "Hell to the no, Steve, get to steppin', Blake, you have thirty seconds. What do you want?"

Steve looked at China with surprise.

"You serious girl?" he asked. "You must be fucking kidding me."

China looked at Steve and growled.

"I don't want nothin' to happen tonight. Please. Get – the fuck – out of here. As my friend, I'm asking you please," she said, gritting her teeth.

"Call me as soon as you leave." Steve turned and walked away.

"Yeah you best get to steppin'!" Blake yelled behind him. Steve didn't even acknowledge his remark.

"What the fuck you want, nigga?" China screamed. "You're gonna act like that to my friends, my co-workers?"

"I thought y'all was fuckin'," Blake said, shrugging.

"So what if we were? That ain't your business anymore,

since you decided to beat the shit out of me."

"China, I already apologized, I got out of control," she cut him off.

"Save the weak excuses for the dumb hoes that'll believe you. I'm done." She turned and started walking away, but Blake grabbed her arm and twirled her to face him again.

"Don't walk away from me, girl."

"Get your goddamn hands off me," she spat, ripping her arm from his grip. She turned and walked away from him. As soon as she was down the street, she hailed a cab. "I'm headed to the arbors? Just go east about 12 blocks and you'll see it. Just stay on this street." Her voice was shaking, and the cabbie looked in his rearview mirror to take a good look at her. Her eyes were vacant and her hand was held to her mouth. He could tell she wanted to cry, but she just kept her eyes focused on the passing buildings.

When China walked in her front door, she made sure to deadbolt her front door, then laid down and poured some Hennessey into a glass with two cubes of ice. Her thoughts turned to church service back in Georgia.

"The light of God surrounds you; the love of God enfolds you; the power of God protects you. And the presence of God watches over you. Wherever you are, God is. Amen."

She never really fell asleep, but she did drink enough to make herself pass out. She was laid flat on the couch, surrounded by an empty bottle of Hennessey, a half-drank bottle of Hpnotiq and a few empty beer cans. In the dead of night, China heard banging on the front door. In her drunken stupor, she stumbled toward the door and started unlocking it.

"I didn't order any pizza," she said, slurring her words and falling backward. She stood right back up and staggered toward the door again. "Hold on, I'm coming."

In her complete drunkenness, she forgot to look through the peephole. When she swung the door open, she saw Blake standing in the entryway. Her eyes widened and her jaw dropped.

"What the – "

"I need to talk to you," Blake said, slurring just as bad as China. They were both hot-mess drunk, each smelling like a busted up liquor store.

"Come on, China." He was quicker and stronger than her, and he pushed his way into her apartment. "I just wanna talk."

"I don't got nothing to say!" She screamed and looked around the room for something to defend herself with. He grabbed her arm and yanked her into his chest.

"I love you," he slurred.

"You don't fuckin' love me," she responded.

"I just want us to be together forever. I want you to have my babies."

"Blake get the fuck outta here! I'm callin the cops," she said.

"You ain't gon' do shit," he said, pushing her by the neck toward the bedroom. "Can't we just have one more time?"

"One more time for what?" she said, her heart beating faster and faster as the seconds went by. "What do you want?"

"I want you," he said, pushing her onto the bed. "I want you so bad." He pulled panties off and put a finger in her sweet spot.

"What are you doing? Stop it, Blake. I don't want you."

"I want you so bad baby. I love you, China."

"Please don't do this, Blake," she pleaded. "Please stop."

Blake ignored her and put another finger inside her. She tried to pry his hands away, but she wasn't strong enough.

"Just relax," he said, continuing to play with her. "Lay back, let me take care of you."

64

China
Doll

"Blake I don't want this, stop."

"OK," he mumbled and removed his hand. Then he grabbed her legs and pinned them up against her chest, eating her out like he was starving to death. "You taste so good, baby. I remember, don't you remember? Call my name. Let me hear you call my name."

He unbuckled his pants and put his penis inside of her, and it wasn't until then that the severity of the moment kicked in.

"Stop it now!" she screamed. "I don't want to do this," she struggled.

"Have my baby, China," he said, pumping into her, still ignoring her pleas.

"Let me go, Blake! Let me go, please!"

He still had her legs pinned to her chest, while he held her by both wrists in one of his hands. She continued to beg for him to stop but he ignored her cries. The more she screamed, the harder he thrust. Tears mixed with mascara were staining the bed sheets.

China Doll

"What are you crying for, baby? You know I love you," he said, tenderly. "I'm getting close baby, I'm gonna come."

Just as he said that, his body tensed, his eyes crossed and he came inside of her.

As soon as she could, China rolled onto her side and wrapped herself in a blanket, crying hysterically.

"Why are you crying baby? You know I love you," Blake said, reaching out to touch her. China slapped his hand away.

"Don't even touch me again," she shrieked.

"What's wrong with you?" he asked.

"Don't act like you don't know! You heard me screaming and crying, you fucking rapist! You're worse than that fucker that ripped your shit open. At least he wasn't telling you he loved you while he raped you. Get the fuck out," she moaned, unable to open her eyes.

Blake tried to recover. "Let me explain."

China opened her eyes and spit in his face.

"You bitch!" He said, standing up. "I come over here to show you how much I love you and you treat me like this?" He leaned down and whispered in her ear. "Why can't you just give in?" China's head was spinning. She shut her eyes tight and pretended she was asleep. The trauma of the night, mixed with nearly two quarts of alcohol that she drank made her pass out into a deep sleep.

China Doll

Chapter Eleven

Life or Death

When China opened her eyes, she didn't know where she was. She was still wrapped in the same blanket that she fell asleep in, but she was on a dark brown leather couch. She sat up slowly, completely unaware of her surroundings. She said a giant sixty inch plasma television on the wall, rows of DVDs and every video game system imaginable underneath. The windows were covered with thick black curtains that didn't let any light in at all. She didn't know where she was or how she got there – all she knew was her head was pounding from getting so drunk last night.

Blake walked into the living room.

"You're awake," he said.

"Where the fuck am I?"

"This is my place."

China looked around, not recognizing her surroundings. She'd actually never been to his house before. In fact, she didn't even know where he lived.

"What, is this where you're gonna hide my body?" China was half joking, but she was also half serious. She had no idea what Blake planned to do. Blake rolled his eyes.

"Look, I know I've done a lot of fucked up shit, but I'm trying to show you that I love you."

"So, you rape me, then you kidnap me? What the fuck is wrong with you?" China stood up. "I need to get the fuck out of here."

"China, will you hear me out?"

"Hear you out? Nigga you want me to hear your black ass out? How 'bout I take you out? This shit has got to stop!" China took a step toward the door.

"Baby! Stop. Listen. I know you don't want to hear me right now, but you need to. You have to. I've loved you for so long, and I know sometimes I do some fucked up shit, but you have to trust me that I love you."

"Love me? You wanna stand there and tell me you love me? Boy, you must have mistaken me for some dumb chickenhead bitch."

"No, China, listen! You're not listening!" Blake's voice was rising, never a good sign in China's book. "You're always fuckin' talkin' but you never listen to me!" His hands turned to fists.

China turned and walked toward the kitchen, only steps away.

"Don't walk away from me when I'm talking to you!"

"What do you want me to say, Blake? Huh? What the fuck am I supposed to say after last night?"

"I was outta control. I don't know what I did or why I did it. I was blacked out. Baby you know I love you, I

China
Doll

don't understand why you don't believe me."

"I don't believe you 'cause you keep on doin' fucked up shit to me and you never live up to your word. If you love me, just love me."

"I'm sorry baby," he hung his head and backed up against the wall. Soon, China realized he was crying. Blake slid down to the floor and put his head between his knees. "I really am sorry. You're the only girl that's been down with me, through thick and thin. It's all my fault."

"You're damn right it is," China said, her voice full of accusation.

"I'm gonna lose you, I'm gonna lose the only woman I've ever loved, aren't I?"

"Well," China started to lose her edge. Whenever she saw Blake cry, she started to get weak in the knees. You know it's bad when you see a thug cry. "I think you should've though of that well before you started fuckin' shit up. This is your fault, B. Not mine."

He looked up at her with red eyes.

"I can't do anything right, can I?" Blake asked. "I can't do a damn thing right, can I?"

"Not by me. You ain't never done nothin' right by me. You wanna control me, you wanna hold me down, you wanna beat me, you wanna fuck shit up. No, you can't do nothin' right Blake. And, the worst part? It ain't nobody's fault but yours."

Blake started sobbing.

"You're right. You're right China."

Blake stood up and walked into the bathroom and shut the door behind him. China heard the bathtub water running, so she walked into the living room and turned on the TV. She had no idea where she was, nor did she know how long Blake would be in the bathroom, but she knew one thing: if Blake cried, you knew he wasn't about to get violent. He was more likely to apologize and treat her better – just like he did in Jamaica. Part of her even hoped for another 180 degree turnaround like he pulled on that island. After thirty minutes, China realized the bathwater was still on. She looked back toward the bathroom and realized water was seeping out from underneath the bathroom door.

She took two steps, and then stopped to call out to him.

"Blake?"

No response.

"Blake, are you OK?"

Still, no response. She took a few more steps and put her ear to the bathroom door.

"Blake, you're scaring me. What are you doing?"

This time, when she heard nothing from the other side of the door, she realized something was wrong. Then, as she looked down at her feet, the water that was rushing out from under the door began to run red. Blood red.

"Blake!" China shrieked, "what are you doing?" and tried to open the door. It wasn't locked, but was wedged closed with something. "Blake! Let me in, you're scaring me!"

The water had turned blood red and was running over her bare feet.

She pushed the door as hard as she could, he feet slipping underneath her. It was hard to keep her balance, but her adrenaline was pumping and she eventually had a crack in the door opened, enough for her to poke her head in. As soon as she looked in, she would see something she would never forget.

Blake had put a shelf in front of the door to keep China out, and then drawn a warm bath. Then, he took a razorblade to his wrists. He wasn't his normal color, and his lips that were normally pink, were dark blue.

China pushed past the shelf and jumped into the tub.

"Blake! Blake, baby! No!" She cradled his head in her chest and rocked back and forth.

"Wake up, Blake, wake up," she pleaded, tears streaming down her face. "Blake, please, wake up," she

China
Doll

screamed. Nothing happened.

She ran to the living room and dialed 911. The operator was asking questions, but China was too panicked to listen. "Yes I need an ambulance. My boyfriend just slit his wrists! Blake. Rasheed Blake. Rasheed Blake is his name! Just get here, I need you here now!"

She realized she didn't know where they were, so she ran to the front door.

"We're on the corner of Elm and St. Claire. I think we're on the south side."

She dropped the phone on the couch without hanging up, hoping they could trace the call and find her location with GPS.

When she ran back to the bathroom, Blake's eyes were still vacant, his lips still blue. She turned the faucet off and dived back into the pool of blood that Blake lay in.

"Baby, you have to wake up, I forgive you, I'm sorry," she pleaded, tears streaming from both eyes. "I forgive you, Blake, I forgive you, I forgive you."

Just then, she felt a hand on her shoulder.

"Miss, I need you to get out of the tub." She looked up to see a young man of twenty-five or so, dressed in all blue. The paramedics had arrived.

China sat outside of the bathroom while another paramedic helped get Blake's body out of the bathtub. They carried him to the living room and put him down on the rug. The first started CPR while the second called into dispatch.

"Male, approximately 25-30 years old, apparent suicide."

"Miss, does he have any family?"

"No. He has no one. Just, just me," she said, numbly.

"No parents, no children, nothing?"

"No. Nothing. Just me. All he had was me."

"Miss, there's, I'm sorry but, there's nothing we can do."

China's head fell, but she didn't cry. She didn't have

71

China
Doll

any emotion whatsoever. She crawled across the floor to touch Blake one last time. He was already getting cold.

"I'm sorry," the young paramedic said. "There really was nothing we could do. He was gone before we got here."

China walked into the bathroom to gather Blake's things and saw something she didn't notice before.

She looked at her reflection in the mirror. Just before Blake died, he wrote "I'm sorry," in his own blood.

*China
Doll*

Chapter Twelve

Surprise

China rode with the paramedics to the hospital. They said she needed should get evaluated, just to make sure she was OK. Besides, she didn't really know where she was, and had no way to get home. She wasn't really dressed, either.

"Ma'am, please come with me," the nurse said. China blindly followed before the nurse sat her in a room that wasn't much larger than a prison cell. "The doctor will be with you momentarily," she said.

China looked down at her hands. They still had traces of Blake's blood on them. Tears started to well in her eyes, tears that she didn't even really understand. Blake had beaten her, raped her, and she still was crying for his death?

She should be dancing in the streets, she told herself. But, when all was said and done, she could only think back to Jag, how she fell so in love. After Jag's death, she thought she would never love again, but somehow, someway, she fell in love again.

Now, he heart had been broken again.

China wiped away her tears and threw her head back. "Never again," she said to herself. "From now on, it's just me."

At that very moment, China's doctor walked in and greeted her. The doctor was about forty years old, a dark-skinned black woman with long flowing hair and hazel eyes. She was gorgeous.

"Hello, Ms." She paused, "Ms. Doll. I'm Dr. Jones."

"Hi Doctor. They told me I should come for," she swallowed, "for an evaluation."

"Oh, were you the witness to the suicide?"

"Yes, that, that was me."

The doctor took her pulse, looked in her eyes, her ears and her throat, listened to her breathing and tested her glands.

China
Doll

"This is basically what we'd do for a physical, but I'm noticing some bruising. Have you been involved in an altercation lately?"

"Yes," China said, with down turned eyes. Dr. Jones had seen that look too many times in her career. Bruises on the hands, wrists, thighs and ribcage? It all pointed to abuse, maybe even rape.

"I'm just going to do a little blood work and we'll be done."

She took a small sample and put a hand on China's shoulder. "I'll be right back, sweetheart. Just stay right here. In the meantime, I'll have a nurse bring you some clothes. I assume you're a size, six?"

"Four," China said. "Size four."

Thirty minutes later, China was fully dressed and the Dr. returned.

"Well, I have good news. Your vitals check out. From everything I can tell, you're perfectly healthy."

"Good," China said, picking up her things and taking a step toward the door.

"Wait," Dr. Jones said in a firm tone. "There's something we have to talk about before you leave."

China looked at the doctor and took a deep breath.

"And what might that be?" she asked, with a pointed attitude.

"Well, first of all, you're pregnant."

75

China
Doll

Chapter Thirteen

A New Life

"You're pregnant?" Angie said with wide eyes. "You must be kidding me. I can't believe what I'm hearing. You must be jokin'. You must be."

"Girl, I'm pregnant." China said with a sigh.

"How far along?"

"Dr. Jones said not more than a month or so. I'm not showing yet, and it's so early on that they can't really say."

Angie put her arm around China.

"Shit," Teri said from the back seat of Angie's car. "That's wild. I can't even believe it. Y'all use protection?"

"Barely ever," China said. "Not for a while now."

Teri and Angie had arrived at the hospital earlier to take China home. China had filled both of them in on what had happened that day. Neither were very sad for Blake, but both of them respected China enough to keep their mouths closed.

"So what you gon' do girl, you gon' keep it?"

"I don't know yet. It's too early to talk about all that."

The three sat silently on the 30 minute ride home, until they pulled into China's apartment complex. They walked her to her door and talked for a second. China wanted to be alone.

"Are you sure you don't want company? Chinese food and some corny movie? You shouldn't be alone right now, no one should be alone after what you've been through today.

"OK," China sighed. "Chinese does sound good. Y'all want House of the Dragon from down the street?"

"No, their egg rolls are bunk," Teri said. "How about Hong Kong Palace?"

"Yeah!" Angie said. "Their Kung Pao chicken is the best."

"I'm gonna go inside and change into something comfortable," China said. "I'll come with you, baby," Teri said.

Angie went and got food and a movie while the other two talked in China's bedroom.

"I just can't believe it. First, Blake, now I find out I have this baby? I just, I just can't believe it." China said.

"Everything happens for a reason," Teri offered. "You remember when I was datin' Marcus last year?" China nodded. "He got me pregnant."

China looked like she just saw a ghost.

"When? What, how did that happen?"

"Girl, you know how that happens," Teri said with a giggle.

"I know how it happens, but, what'd you do?"

"I got rid of it. You and I both know I'm in no shape to take care of a baby. I couldn't bring another life into this world if all I could ever give it was pain. I wasn't ready. I had to be grown up enough to know that."

China nodded again.

"I'm not telling you what to do, I'm just telling you my experience. To each their own. You know I'll respect and support whatever decision you make. You're like my sista."

One tear fell from China's eye before she stood up and made her way to the kitchen sink for a glass of water.

"I know. I guess I just have a lot of decisions to make."

Just then, Angie popped in the door with food and movies.

"I got 'Bad Boys,' and 'Bad Boys II,'" she said. "I figured, when all else fails, get somethin' with Will Smith."

The girls gave a small laugh and sat on the couch. For the first time in days, China felt safe.

79

China
Doll

Chapter Fourteen

Choices

The next day, China got up early and went to work like nothing had ever happened.

"Just get back into the swing of things, China. Just keep moving forward. Whatever you do, don't stop pushin'," Angie told her. That was some of the best advice China ever got.

Steve was the only person at work she told about the situation, and he was as understanding as all of his other friends.

"I still love your crazy ass," was his only response. After work, he took her out for dinner at her favorite Mexican place, Rancho Fiesta.

"So, what's the plan?" he asked.

"Shit, I don't know. I just wish I could have a margarita," she said with a laugh.

"Well if you ever need anything, just let me know what you need."

"Thanks, Steve. That means a lot. I think I'm going to keep it, I don't think I can handle any other death in my life. That, and this baby's going to be the only thing that'll remind me of Blake."

"Is that something you want to remember? You want a memory of that man in your life?"

"Say what you will, Steve, but Blake loved me. He went through a lot in his life, and he was really fucked up, but deep down, I really think he loved me."

"China, I met him. That wasn't love, that was something else."

"Steve, please, don't. I'm not ready to talk about him like that yet."

Steve looked shocked. "I understand, babygirl. Don't even sweat it."

They sat at the restaurant and talked for hours before Steve took her home.

"Be good, China. Call me if you need anything. I mean it. Anything."

"Thanks Steve. I'll see you at work on Monday."

Steve gave her a kiss on the cheek and drove away. When China walked into her apartment, she took one look around and broke down crying. She realized it was time to clean house.

She tore through all of her old clothes. Anything that Blake ever bought her went into a black plastic garbage bag that she wanted to take to the homeless shelter to donate to them. She couldn't look at anything that would remind her of Blake.

She walked back into her closet and started sorting through her shoes. When she reached for a pair of Manolos, she saw an unfamiliar black bag, tucked underneath a box.

"What the fuck," she said out loud.

She pulled one of the straps and out came a large duffle bag. She immediately started crying, wondering what she would find inside. It was easily eighty pounds, and took most of China's strength to drag it onto her bed. As soon as it was on her bed, she looked at it like it was a poisonous snake.

She sat at the foot of her bed and took a deep breath, She pulled the zipper open slowly, and looked inside.

What she found inside made her stomach turn and eyes bulge out like Bugs Bunny.

Money, and lots of it. She pulled out stack after stack of $100 bills, searching for anything else. No note, no explanation, nothing else in the bag except stack after stack of bills.

"Oh my God!" she screamed, trembling. How much could there be?

There had to have been more than $3 million in $100 bills, but she stopped counting after a while. All she knew was that she'd never have to work again. She also found a small pistol at the bottom of the bag, fully loaded. It was small enough to conceal anywhere on her body – so she figured Blake had meant for her to have it.

That night, she took everything Blake ever bought her to charities and went straight to the airport. When she got to the counter, she knew exactly what she wanted.

"I need a one-way ticket to Jamaica," he said.

"When would you like to fly out?" he asked with a friendly tone.

"Get me there tonight," she answered. "Money is no object."

Chapter Fifteen

Release

China Doll

By the time China arrived in Jamaica, she was running on fumes. She'd had a shitty week and she just wanted to rest. As soon as she stepped off the plane and smelled the warm island breeze, she was instantly revived. Her first stop was the beach. China stepped into the waves and spread her arms, soaking up as much sunshine as she could. She felt the sand between her toes, and the cool saltwater rushed against her ankles. She felt like she was in heaven.

She left the beach and walked to the closest resort she could find. The closest resort, luckily, was less than 100 yards from where she was standing.

"Hello, I need a room. A room with the biggest bed you

have in this whole damn hotel!" she said with a smile.

"Absolutely," the man behind the counter said. "Would you like one bed or two?"

"Oh, I'm alone. I just need one bed."

The man behind the counter licked his lips.

"A pretty lady like you, alone in Jamaica? Very dangerous," he said, clicking his tongue and winking at her with a grin. "Very, very dangerous."

"Oh, I can take care of myself," China said. "Always have."

"I see. Well we'll put you in master suite A. Top floor, to the left. Do you need help with your luggage?" he asked in a sexy accent.

"This is all I have, I think I can make it," she said, patting her bag. Before she left, China packed only one bag, the contents of which were a sundress, bathing suit and some things to give herself a manicure and pedicure. Oh, and stacks upon stacks of cash.

China Doll

Once she got to her room, she realized how amazing it was. A wraparound view of the island, stocked refrigerator, big screen televisions on every wall, a full kitchen, and her favorite part: a jacuzzi.

"This is the life!" she squealed, before laying down on the plush bed. She reached for the phone and ordered room service. Fifteen minutes later, the man from the front desk arrived with her food.

"Hello, pretty lady," he said again, with a grin.

"Hello," China said. "Nice to see you again."

He flashed his pearly whites at her.

"You have beautiful teeth," she said, with a 'come hither' look.

He let out a barely audible laugh. "I thank you, you are very beautiful yourself." His eyes sparkled. He promptly turned around and shut the door behind him.

China took her food out to the balcony and dined in the sunshine, while daydreaming about her new life. As soon as she was daydreaming about her life, she realized she was also daydreaming about the man from the hotel, and she didn't even know his name.

"What the hell is wrong with me?" she thought. "Am I just a horny-ass bitch or what?" She laughed to herself. Then, all she could picture was his hand running up and down her body, his other hand stroking her hair, his full lips kissing hers, their bodies rolling through the sand and surf. She wanted him to fuck the shit out of her. She had to do something to get her mind off of him.

She dialed Teri's number.

"Teri, guess where the fuck I am."

"Where?" she said, worried.

"Jamaica."

"What? Girl you must be fuckin' with me."

"Girl, I ain't fuckin' with nobody," she said, laughing.

"You scandalous bitch. What you gonna do about work?"

"I told Steve about the whole thing, he'll explain it to them for me. He told me to take a few weeks off for me."

"Probably the best idea," she agreed.

"So what's up in Jamaica?" Teri asked.

"Honestly, I can't get my mind off this guy who works here at the hotel. Oh my God is he fine." China wasn't holding back.

"Well maybe you should go exploring. You know, take your mind off everything that's happened in the past few days."

"Maybe you're right," China said, seriously considering fucking the shit out of the sexiest Jamaican man she's ever seen.

"Well, it better be worth it."

"Shit, you'd know I'd fuck him if I could," Teri said, laughing.

"Girl, I know you would. You'd fuck anything with a dick!"

"China, you know me too well. Seriously though. Have

some fun, get your mind off everything that's botherin' you. Take some time to make yourself happy, OK?"

"Teri, you're right. Thanks babygirl. I'll call you soon."

China hung up the phone and put the dirty dishes outside of her door. She'd not slept much in the past few days, so she stripped down and laid on the bed. Her thoughts went back to the dark Jamaican, and her fingers began to caress her sensitive spots. She moaned slightly as she pushed one finger at a time in between her thighs, all of the sudden, she remembered why she was in Jamaica – because of Blake's money. She was carrying Blake's baby. Now she wanted to fuck some other man? She got sick to her stomach, so she rolled over and put her head on the softest pillow she's ever touched. She was asleep as soon as her head touched that pillow.

88

China
Doll

The next day, she took a taxi in to town to buy gifts and souvenirs. After that, she lounged by the pool, had lunch at a cute local restaurant, and wandered back to the hotel. By the time sunset hit, she was starting to lose her mind. She didn't want to be in Jamaica, she didn't want to go home, she didn't know what the hell to do with herself. All she wanted was some security.

She walked to the lobby of the hotel, hoping to find the dark attendant she'd had so many fantasies about. She didn't see him at the counter, so she turned around and headed for the elevator. As soon as the elevator arrived, she stepped into it without looking. Just as she did, she faceplanted into his chest.

"Oh my God, I'm so sorry!" She said, completely embarrassed.

"It is OK, pretty lady," he said. "No worries." He walked right by her.

"Wait," she said. "I never caught your name," she said, seductively.

"My name," he took a breath, "my name is Jerome."

"Well, it's nice to meet you, Jerome," she said.

"Where are you off to?" he inquired, "If I may ask."

"I, um, I'm going, uh," she collected herself. "I'm going back to my room to relax. I've been out all day."

"Alone?" he asked, hypnotizing her with his words. "What's a girl like you doing here alone?" At this point, there was no mistaking the fact that he was flirting with her.

"I came to get away. I have a man back home. I just needed some space. I've only been here a short time," she said, rambling.

"Listen, why don't you let me take you out in a few hours, after my shift? Let me show you my home."

China batted her eyes.

"Go to your suite, get dressed, and I'll come get you around ten." China didn't respond.

"I won't take no for an answer," he said with the sexiest smile she'd seen in a long time.

Walking to her room, she began to question herself again. "You can't go out with this man," she told herself. "You're not ready." She started to pace.

She turned the shower on and picked out the perfect white Bebe dress, silver Via Spiga sandals and diamond jewelry. She pinned her hair back into a messy bun, applied a little MAC lip gloss and sprayed herself liberally with DKNY Be Delicious.

Then came the knock on her door. Even though she looked like a million dollars, she was still nervous.

"Hey," she said, greeting him at the door.

"Hello," he replied, extending his hand. "You look beautiful."

She smiled, following him out of the room.

"Where are we going?" she asked.

"For a walk on the beach so you can tell me all about

yourself."

He didn't try to take her hand. Instead, he held the door open and gestured for her to move toward the exit closest to the beach. Once they were outside, it was only a short walk to open sand and water.

"Well, what do you want to know?" She leaned on him and took her shoes off.

"Everything." He looked sincere.

"Well, I'm China. China Doll. I'm from Atlanta, but I live in Baltimore. I work with at-risk kids, I'm 26 years old, and have no man."

"Nice to meet you, China," he said with a smirk. "I'm Jerome. Jerome Lee. I'm from Kingston. I work here at the resort. I'm 29 years old, and have no kids and no woman."

"Well, it's nice to meet you, Jerome," she said with a wink.

They walked along the beach, sharing stories of childhood and their goals as adults.

China
Doll

"I plan to move to New York sometime this year to go back to school. You yanked don't realize the opportunities you have, living in the states."

"Yankees?" She asked.

Jerome laughed. "Yes, you Americans."

"What do you want to go to school for?"

"Business," he said. "I got my bachelor's degree at the University College of Caribbean, but I haven't been able to do much with it here. Now, I'm working here at the resort and two other places to make enough money to get out of here.

"So you have three jobs?" she laughed. "I guess it's true what they say about Jamaicans."

Jerome laughed too. "I know I have to do to get where I want to be. If that means working three jobs, that's that I have to do. How long are you here in Jamaica?"

"I'm not sure yet. I bought a one-way ticket, so I guess I can stay as long as I want." Jerome smiled, but his eyes looked worried. "Oh, it's getting so late," China said, looking at her watch.

"The sun will be up in a few hours. Thank you for spending the night with me," he said. "I enjoy your company."

China wasn't used to spending time with a man this nice. She automatically assumed there was something behind what he was saying, but his eyes were so genuine, she put it out of her mind.

"Do you want to come in for a while, to, you know, finish our conversation?"

"I'd be delighted," he said, readily accepting her invitation. He walked her to her room and grabbed a spot on her couch. "Join me," he said, patting the cushion where he wanted China to join him.

"You know, I thought I would be so sleepy, but I don't feel a tired bone in my body," China said.

"It's the sea air. It rejuvenates."

"I think you're right. So, can I get you something to drink?"

"You have a Red Stripe?" He asked.

"In fact," she paused, searching the contents of the refrigerator. "I do!" She popped the top on the Jamaican beer and sat right down next to Jerome.

"You smell so good," he said, getting closer to China.

"Thank you. And, thank you for letting me talk your ear off all night."

"It was nothing," she said. Just then, he leaned in and kissed her on the lips. She pulled back. "I'm sorry. I didn't," she trailed off and looked deeply into his eyes. She realized she needed this. She needed the physical contact, she needed Jerome, right or wrong, she needed this, just for tonight.

Jerome laid her on the bed and planted sweet kisses all over her body. "May I?" he asked before lifting her dress.

She licked his lips with her tongue. Softly, Jerome

stroked her thighs and kissed her, plunging his thick, juicy tongue deep into her mouth. She helped him remove her panties and stretched one leg over his shoulders. She pushed his face between her thighs.

"Please, kiss it."

Taking her lead, Jerome teased her clit with his tongue. In and out, he dipped his tongue seductively. Her hips adopted the pace of his rhythm. She shuddered in delight and grabbed his hand, placing his fingers in her mouth so she could suck each one. She licked his palm, tickling it, tasting him.

"I'm almost there," she moaned, about to reach her climax. "Oh my God Jerome," she started breathing deeply.

"I don't want you to come yet," he said. He stood up and stripped naked. The magnificent body standing before her was like a black Greek god. She was captivated. He palmed her breasts and sucked each one, taking time to pay attention to each nipple. He stomach was next, with kisses and licks covering the surface, and then placed soft kisses on each thigh.

"You are beautiful," he purred. He kissed the back of her knees and each calf, making his way to her feet. He took each foot in her mouth, licking and kissing each of her toes, sweet and sexy at the same time. Then, he moved slowly up her thighs and continued in the spot where her legs met. Then he flipped her over. He grabbed her hips and raised her up to where his rock-hard member was waiting.

"Jerome," China called. "Jerome, please take me, make me feel good."

He raised his body and entered her slowly.

"I'm so wet!" she moaned, and moved in sync with Jerome. "Can you feel how wet I am? I'm so ready for you."

Jerome's large dick rammed in between her thighs, and China let out a gasp. "Oh my God, you're everything

92

China Doll

I imagined you to be."

He held her close to him while he slowly hit every one of her spots. She wrapped her arms around his neck, enjoying every minute.

Unexpectedly, Jerome picked her up off the bed while still inside of her and palmed her ass. He lifted her up and down on his dick.

"Jerome!" she yelled.

He thrust himself deeper inside her.

"Nigga you got me so open!" Tears began to fall down her face. She felt like she was in heaven. No man, not even Jag, ever got her to that place before. "I'm coming, I'm coming, she cried out. She reached her third or fourth climax, and then Jerome released himself inside of her.

"I beat you," she smiled as she lay in his strong arms.

"This time," he teased.

"I'm going to take a shower. Join me?" She asked, standing up and slinking toward the bathroom. They took a long, sensual, sexy shower together.

China Doll

"Your skin is so soft," Jerome said as he planted sweet kisses all over her body. "I could stay here and love you all day and night."

She smiled at him.

"But I've got to work, beautiful," he said as he placed one last deep, scintillating kiss on her lips. "Will I see you again? He asked as she stepped out of the shower.

"Do you want to?" She teased.

"Of course," he smiled as he put on his pants.

"We'll see," she replied while walking him to the door.

"Well, then, until next time," he said.

She watched him walk down the hallway and then closed the door when he disappeared behind the elevator doors. As she lay in bed reliving those erotic hours, she didn't even feel one drop of remorse in her entire body. It was exactly what she needed.

For the next week, Jerome and China were like a new

couple. She waited for him to get off work, and they spent every night together. They talked for hours. With Jerome, China could express every one of her true feelings about home. She confided in him more than she could in most of her friends, except Teri and Angie. No one ever took as much time with China as Jerome, and she loved every minute of it.

"Let's go to Kingston," he suggested.

"Don't you have to work?"

"No problem, mon," he responded.

Then, Jerome whisked her away for a pleasure-filled day in Kingston. They snorkled, lounged on the beach and even swam with dolphins.

"Let me take you to my favorite restaurant," he suggested excitedly.

"I'd love to go," she told him

She couldn't get enough of him – his eyes, his smile, his body, all of it. Once they were seated in the restaurant, China realized how lucky she was. She could hear the ocean waves beating against the shore right outside the window, and a warm, tropical breeze drifted in and wrapped itself around her bare shoulders.

China
Doll

"I enjoy spending time with you," he said sincerely. His large, muscular hands caressed hers. Lovingly, he inserted each of her fingers into his mouth and sucked on them. The sweet spot between her legs became so wet, and pulsed so wildly, that she was almost uncomfortable.

"I enjoy you too."

"I've never met anyone like you, China. I think about you all day. I wait to see you all day, every day."

"You're reading my mind," she smiled. "It's been a long time since I've had this much fun."

Everything seemed to be going well with Jerome, but there was still one secret that China couldn't tell him about: the baby that was slowly growing inside of her.

The next night, as they were sitting at a bar, Jerome ordered two cocktails – one for each of them.

"Oh, I don't drink," China said, shying away from the glass.

"You don't drink? You must be kidding. I don't know anyone who doesn't drink. Come on, taste it."

China was all too conscious about the hazards of drinking while pregnant. "No, I'm perfectly fine without it. Really." She said, moving the glass away from with the back of her hand. Jerome looked at her like she was from outer space, and quickly downed both drinks.

"What shall we do tonight, my doll?" he asked.

"Oh, I don't know. I think I just want to go chill in my room."

"Oh that's too bad. I wanted to take you somewhere special."

"No, that's OK," she said. All of the sudden, she could feel vomit rising in her throat. "This must be what morning sickness feels like," she told herself. "Listen, Jerome, I really need to go to bed. I need to rest or somethin'. All the sudden I'm feelin' all nasty."

"OK China. Let's take you back to your room." He picked her up and noticed she was very warm. "I think you have a fever," he said. "You are feeling very warm."

All of the sudden, China started feeling dizzy, and her legs let out from beneath her. Thankfully, Jerome caught her.

"Sorry," she laughed. "Must be the sun."

When China was back in her room, the pains intensified. She started to feel like she was in labor. She was all alone, with no one else in the world to come to her rescue. Jag was gone, Blake was gone, and all of her friends were in another country. All she knew to do was call Jerome. She screamed into the phone: "Jerome! I need you here now. Something is wrong!"

Jerome sounded shocked and worried, mostly because he had no idea what was happening.

"Get here, please," she shrieked. "Please!"

China crawled her way to the bathroom and threw

up in the toilet. She felt like her gut was tearing itself apart. When she moved, she noticed blood where she was sitting.

"Oh my God, no." She started praying. "Please God, please keep me alive through this. Please help me, please help me," she kept repeating. A few seconds later, Jerome burst through the door.

"China!" he yelled, noticing the trail of blood that led to her on the bathroom floor. "What is happening?"

"I don't know!" she screamed, "Please, get help.

Jerome ran to the phone at the bedside and called the front desk.

"Listen, it's Jerome. I'm in China's suite. China Doll, yes. Top floor. Send a doctor! Now goddammit!" he growled fiercely into the receiver.

"China, we have a doctor on staff here at the resort. You'll be fine, he's on his way."

China
Doll

The doctor, a friend of Jerome's since childhood, flew into the bathroom in less than five minutes. He gave China a sedative and some painkillers. He knew exactly what was going on, and he knew there was nothing he could do to stop it.

"China, you're having a miscarriage," the doctor said. Jerome's eyes got wide and his jaw dropped. China never told him about being pregnant. Now he knew why China wouldn't ever drink with him.

"The bleeding has stopped, so you're going to be fine. There's nothing we could've done. Sometimes this happens. It's natural. You'll be fine."

China started silently weeping.

"Take me to bed," she said quietly. The two men hoisted her up and took her clothes off before placing her between the sheets. "China, we need to get you cleaned up first," the doctor said. They put her in the bath and tenderly washed her clean. The whole time, she was completely numb to the experience. She had lost the child that Blake gave her – and it was the final link to him. Now, she had nothing left of Rasheed Blake, nothing but a bag full of money.

"I need to sleep," she said with no emotion. "Put me to bed."

Again, they lifted her up and wrapped her in linens.

"I will come back later tonight to check on you, China," Jerome said. "Do not worry, I will return."

China fell asleep wondering if her baby would've been a boy or a girl.

97

China
Doll

Chapter Sixteen

Back to One

When China woke up the next morning, she realized she'd been sleeping for over 16 hours. She still felt terrible, and her entire midsection was in searing pain, but better than it was the day before.

She took a look around the room. Everything looked different. Even the views from the windows didn't look the same. She walked into the living room and found Jerome asleep on the couch.

"Jerome," she said, lightly touching his shoulder. "Baby, wake up." The sunlight was reflecting off of every muscle in his upper body, glistening with his shirt off. His eyes opened.

"China, you're awake."

"Yeah, feelin' like shit though."

Jerome smiled. "Well, it's good to see you awake. Come, sit with me," he said. China sat down right beside him and brought her legs to her chest.. "So, you were pregnant?" He asked, hesitantly.

"Yes. I was pregnant, in case you missed it." She copped an attitude.

"I'm sorry, I just, why didn't you tell me?" he stuttered.

"Oh, you know, you meet a beautiful Jamaican God, you usually don't lead with 'oh, hey, did I mention I was knocked up?' It's pretty personal. Not exactly the kind of thing you share on a first date."

"I thought we were getting pretty personal." His accent was thick because he was so upset.

China Doll

"Well, it's something I wasn't even sure how to deal with. Now, it's gone. I'm just taking it day by day," she said. "I don't know what the fuck I'm doing here anyway. I'm sitting in Jamaica while my entire fuckin' life is in Baltimore, thousands of miles away – across an ocean for fucks sake. Do you know how hard it is to be so far from everyone and everything you've ever known?"

"No, I've spent my entire life on the island. I told you that."

"OK, well get off of my case. I can't just abandon all of my responsibilities and live in some island paradise fantasy world for the rest of my life. I need to get back to the real world."

"This is my real world." He looked like a dog that had been beaten down.

"I know it's your world, J. It's just not mine. I've got to go, I've got to get my life back together. I've got to get myself back on track. I left my home, my friends, everything I've ever known for a fantasy. I've got to get back. You know it and I know it. There was no way I could stay here forever, anyway. I'm living in your hotel, dammit! You knew the money had to run up at some point."

"I know," he said quietly, looking down. "I don't know how to respond."

"We had fun. Isn't that enough?"

A fire lit behind Jerome's eyes. "I am surprised at you, Miss Doll," he said, rolling his neck from side to side. "I never thought you could be so cold. You have ice in your veins or what? You come here, we talk about our lives, we have conversations that go all night, we stare into each others' eyes. That is real, China. That is real life. That's the kind of thing that people look for their whole lives. And now you just want to throw it all away? You say you want to go home for yourself, but I think you want to go home because you are scared. Scared of living, scared of yourself and scared of love!"

China looked shocked at Jerome's accusation. She had no words to respond.

"Look, I need to pack, I need to get out of here. I've got to go."

Jerome sat silently. "You're right. You do need to go. You need to get off my island."

"No, Jerome, stop it."

"Stop it? Stop what? I have duties I need to tend to," he said, grabbing his shirt and throwing it on over his head. "Time for me to go."

He walked toward the door and opened it a crack. "China," he said with his back to her. "One thing."

She waited silently.

"Make me a promise. Never ever settle for something you don't want. Go after what you want. Use the fire inside you. Goodbye, China." He didn't turn around to look at her and he didn't give her a kiss goodbye. He just stepped out and closed the door behind him.

Chapter Seventeen

Home Sweet Home

As soon as China landed, she called Teri and Angie to come pick her up at the airport. Flaunting her sun kissed body, China emerged from the plane looking like a goddess. She was wearing a handmade Jamaican gown, a seashell necklace, and diamond earrings. Angie and Teri couldn't even believe their eyes.

"Damn, girl. Lookin' like a Black Goddess all the sudden. Why you look so good?" Angie asked.

"Jamaica always does that for me. It's like the fountain of youth. Everything about that place is just amazing," China said, with stars in her eyes.

"Well lets go get some food," Teri suggested.

"I could eat a whole pig," China said. "Let's get

somethin' as soon as we damn well can!" They all walked toward the parking lot, laughing.

As soon as they got on the road, China recounted everything about Jamaica – all the details, except the miscarriage. She told them about the beaches, the people, the sex with Jerome. She poured her heart out about everything. When they got to their favorite barbecue joint, China ordered a Red Stripe.

"Makes me feel like I'm back in Jamaica," she said.

"Girl, you know you can't drink," Angie said.

"Put that down right now!" Teri said. "What the fuck you think you're doin'?"

China shook her head back and forth. "Um, that's the one thing I didn't tell you about. I, I lost the baby," she said quietly.

The girls sat in silence.

"When? What happened?"

"Day before yesterday," China said with downcast eyes. "I didn't do anything wrong, it just happened. The doctor said these things happen all the time."

"Well, it's probably for the best. Did you really want a walking reminder of the man who raped and beat you?" Teri said. China shot her the look of death.

"Girl, I just got back. Don't start on me already."

"OK, OK, we get it. Let's move on."

They sat together for an hour while China described the wonderful paradise she left.

"Part of me never wants to leave, but I just can't convince myself to just set up shop on an island and leave my entire life behind," she thought out loud.

*China
Doll*

When Teri dropped Angie off at her place, she looked at China with serious eyes.

"You care if I come over?"

"Hell naw, girl. What's up?"

"Just wanna get some stuff out. Seems like after all the honesty we been killin' today, might as well go for it all."

They made the trip across town and finally pulled into China's place.

As they walked in, Teri started spilling her guts.

"I really wanted to confess something to you, China. Something that has been on my mind for a minute now."

China started to worry.

"What's up girl?"

"You've got to promise to be calm."

"Right, but you'd better start spillin' before I start flippin' a bitch."

"I understand, but I'm tellin' you, I need your support now. I need you as a friend."

"Teri!" China yelled. "Could you get to the damn point already? Shit." China rolled her eyes.

"Well, OK. You should know I haven't told anyone about this, not even Angie, so you gotta keep your mouth shut. Got it?"

"Yeah."

"We clear?"

"Crystal."

"I cheated on Kurt."

China whirled around and looked at her, then stepped back and sat down on the couch.

"Nigga what?"

"I cheated. I cheated on Kurt. It's been tearing me up inside and I don't know what to do."

"What? When did you do it, and who with?" China asked. "You know if he finds out he's gonna flip the fuck out, right?"

"I know, I know."

"So who was it?"

"That's not important. But, there is something else."

"What?" China said, confident that she already knew the answer.

China
Doll

"I'm," she stopped and took a breath. "Well, I'm pregnant."

"And you don't know who the babydaddy is." China said bluntly.

"No, I, I really don't." Teri started crying. China dropped the line of questioning because she could see how upset her friend was.

"If this baby comes out lookin' like some other man, you're fucked. You do know that, right? You've got to tell him before he finds out on his own."

Teri sniffled. "I don't know how. How am I supposed to tell him that not only did I fuck some other man, but I might have someone else's baby? China, he'd leave me!"

"Leave you, he might beat yo' ass," China blurted out. "But who cares, you just gotta stay healthy. I decided to leave the country and start bangin' some Jamaican pool boy, and you see where that got me. Almost took me to the hospital."

"I know, I know."

"I'll go with you to tell him."

"China, if you would, that'd be amazing, please."

"Anything you need, babygirl. Just let me know."

"Alright, well I should run home. I have so much shit to get done before tomorrow."

"Gotcha. Well, call me if you need anything, OK?"

"Thanks girl," Teri said. She gave China a peck on the cheek and drove home.

Chapter Eighteen

No More Secrets

Months went by and Teri still hadn't told Kurt that there was a possibility that the baby wasn't his. China tried to offer as much support as she could, but nothing seemed to help. Teri was a wreck.

"You're gonna have to say something. It's not healthy for you or the baby. You don't eat, you barely sleep, you've got to be more careful!

She ignored China. "Are you trying to lose that baby, Teri?"

"What the fuck are you talking about?"

"I'm just sayin', you best take care of yourself or somethin' could happen. Learn from my mistakes."

"China, you don't get it."

"Then help me get it, Teri! Damn!" For some reason, she wouldn't let China in. China could only feel like her friend was shutting her down, keeping her at a distance. She could tell there was more going on in Teri's head other than a baby. Her visits became more and more infrequent, until she was seeing her sometimes once a week or not at all.

One night, after midnight, there was a frantic knock on the door. China went to the door and looked through the peephole. It was Teri.

When she opened the door, she realized that Teri was in full-out panic mode, tears streaming down her cheeks, eyes red from what looked like hours of crying.

"China, I can't hold it inside anymore," she cried.

"Come inside, Teri. What the fuck you doin' here so late?"

"I can't hold it inside. I have to tell you. I'm sorry, I'm so sorry."

China
Doll

"What's wrong? Teri I don't understand, talk to me."

"I can't say it! I can't fuckin' say it," she said, Teri was completely hysterical, barely able to breathe.

"What happened? What the fuck is going on?"

"I," she paused and gathered herself, "I had sex with Blake."

China froze.

"You best say that one more time so I can make sure I'm hearing you correctly."

"I, I slept with, I slept with Blake," she muttered.

China stopped dead in her tracks.

"You did what?"

"I had sex with him."

"For how long?"

"We were together for about six months before he died."

"Did you fuck him just once, or like, on the regular?" China was getting ready to lose it.

"On the reg."

"I can't fucking believe it!" China completely lost it. "You come in here, like you're my fuckin' friend, and you're tellin' me that you were fuckin' my man? And, oh wait, let me guess, that fuckin' bastard child you're carrying around, that might be his. Am I right?"

Teri didn't say anything.

"I asked you a question you skank bitch!" China screamed.

Teri sat silently. China wound up and slapped her across the face so hard that Teri few backward.

"China! I'm sorry!" Teri squealed.

"Oh hell no, you ain't half as sorry as I'm about to make you. You're a low-down dirty ho, you know that? Fuckin' piece of fucking garbage! If you weren't pregnant, I'd be pounding your face into the ground right now. I'd show you 'hood' Teri. Oh I'd fuckin' show you!"

China felt like vomiting.

"Please, please forgive me," Teri cried. "Please, let me make it OK."

*China
Doll*

"Make it OK? Bitch you must be jokin'. You can't expect to just roll up to my house and admit something like that. I never wanna see your skank-ass face again. Never. Next time I see you, you best hope you're still pregnant. As soon as you pop that little crack baby out yo' pussy, your ass is mine. You're – going – down." China was hysterical, seeing red.

"Get the fuck out my house!"

"China, please, can we talk about this?" China backhanded Teri across the face as hard as she could. "We ain't got a goddamn thing to talk about. You're out. Gone. Get to steppin'. Get the fuck outta here."

She ran out of China's apartment and jumped in her car. China was on the phone to Angie before Teri could get out of the parking lot.

She recounted the entire story to Angie, ending the conversation with "I bet she fucked Tommy too, that fuckin' skank-ass piece of trash."

Angie was in her car to pick up China before the end of the conversation. In ten minutes, they were in Teri's driveway, walking toward the door. They didn't knock, they just busted in the front door to find Teri sitting on the couch, alone, crying.

Angie looked at her square in the face.

"Now I'm gonna cut right to the motherfuckin' chase. We cousins, so I'm gonna give you one time to tell me the truth. Have you ever, and I mean ever, slept with my man?"

Teri didn't look up from the couch, but she slowly nodded her head.

"Yes," she confessed softly.

Before she could lift her head up, Angie slapped her across the face. "We're family!" she screamed. "I used to take up for your ass when bitches would say you were a whore. Now, now that I've heard all the stories? I realize you are a fuckin' ho. Street-trash bullshit-ass fuckin' skank-ass ho!"

Angie slapped her again, but harder this time. Teri's hands shot up to her face, then she raised her hand to hit Angie back. That's when China stepped in, grabbing her arm to protect Angie.

"Teri, you outta be glad you're pregnant, otherwise I'd kick the ever-loving shit outta you," Angie said coldly.

"Angie, I'm sorry. You have to believe me, it was a mistake! Teri tried to convince Angie.

"A mistake? How the fuck you gon' tell me it was a mistake? How do you accidentally fuck somebody else's man? What, you trip and fall and end up slurpin' on his dick? That's some fuckin' bullshit and you fuckin' know it!" Everyone in the room was beyond hysterical. "You don't do that kinda shit to family! You'd better hope I don't see you in the streets 'cause my foot'll be in your ass. Don't even try me."

"Was it worth it? Was gettin' that dick worth fuckin' up everyone's life?"

110

China
Doll

"China, I never meant to hurt you!"

"Yes, you did. I believe that's exactly what you were trying to do. You were supposed to be my friend. I thought I could count on you for the rest of my life, but you came into my home and destroyed everything. Did you think about me when you were fucking Blake? Did you see my face? Did you think about the family you crossed when you fucked Tommy, and how bad you'd hurt your cousin, your blood, Angie? It wasn't enough that you had a man; you needed to know you could get ours, too. What you don't realize is you're the one who looks like that whore. Tommy could give a fuck about you and Blake's dead! How's that feel, you dumb bitch? How's it fuckin' feel?"

China turned around and walked toward the door. "Let's go, Angie," she said. "Oh, and Teri? Watch out. You got yours comin'."

"Take me to the block," Angie said in a whisper.

"You sure you wanna air your business like that, babygirl?"

"Just take me to the block, she said again with more force than before.

China drove to the block where she knew Tommy would be. "I got your back," China said as she and Angie jumped out of the car.

"Can I talk to you for a minute?" She asked Tommy in a nasty tone.

"What you doin' out here, boo?" You know you ain't got no business out here. Can't this wait 'til I get home?" He asked.

"Tommy, we're gonna talk now!" she screamed in his face, drawing more attention to herself.

Tommy grabbed her by the arm and took her down the street away form the crowd. China made sure to stay close by so she could hear what was going on.

"I didn't fuck that bitch! She came at me, but I never fucked her," Tommy said.

"Yes, you did! And then you throw salt in the wound

China
Doll

by standing here and lying to me? Why would you do this to me, Tommy? I thought you were better than that. All that shit you talked about moving us out of Baltimore and starting somewhere fresh, that was all bullshit, wasn't it? You were worried about me for a second, cause you was too busy fuckin' my cousin!" Angie was screaming loud enough so every damn person on the block could hear.

She started to walk away from Tommy and then turned back to face him. "I wanted to tell you that I'm pregnant, but since you might have another baby on the way, it shouldn't make any difference." Angie flipped him the middle finger and walked away.

"Stupid ass," China said to Tommy. "You done fucked everything up." China was a bit surprised to hear that Angie was pregnant. She never knew in the first place, so this was news to her.

Angie spent the whole way home on her cell phone with Tommy. The conversation was heated, and never really got resolved. China was doing her best to just block it out and focus on the road.

"Thank you, China," Angie said before she got out of the car at her house. "I have no idea what I'm gonna do."

China understood what she was talking about.

"Well, you have to have it. You have to have the baby."

"I don't know, I have a lot to think about. Thanks again, mama. I'll see you later."

China was glad the drama was nearing a close. She had no energy left to spend on that kind of shit. She needed to get back to work, get back into the swing of things, get back to herself and get her life back on track. Her life had been a living hell for so long, she knew it was time to turn it around. Now, with the amount of cash she had, she could make it all possible.

There was just one matter left. One last loose string to tie up, and that was finding the people who killed Jag, and make them pay. Make them pay dearly.

Later that night, while laying in bed, China heard her phone vibrate.

"Hello?" she answered, half asleep.

"Girl, I wanted to let you know that some shit is goin' down tonight. I just heard from Ray Ray that Tommy is on some crazy shit.

"Wait, what the fuck? Who's Ray Ray?"

"Girl, shit ain't important. What's important is that Tommy is on some crazy shit and he wants to make niggas pay."

"What's he gon' do?" China asked in disbelief.

"I don't know, but whatever it is, it's goin' down tonight. They're bein' all secretive, but I know for a fact it's tonight."

"What could they be doin?"

"I'm on my way over."

China hung up the phone and looked at the clock. The clock next to her bed read 12:15. She couldn't believe all this was going down. Ten minutes later, she heard frantic knocking at the front door.

"Oh my God, China, turn on the news."

"Why? What's goin' on?"

"Turn on channel eight. I just got a message from one of my girls from the block. Somethin' bad went down.

China flipped on the television and tuned it to the right channel.

"Oh my God," China said, dropping the remote control.

What they saw on the television screen were wild flames roaring out of control. It was Teri's house. They had both been there a million times and could recognize it anywhere. The newscaster was blabbering about how they didn't know what happened, but the quickness with which the fire overtook the building, that meant arson.

"Oh my God. You don't think Tommy could've done anything like this, do you?"

"Bitch, you must underestimate Tommy. That nigga is fuckin' grade-A crazy. Loony tunes. Fucked in the head."

Just then, after everything we'd seen, they wheeled a body in a black bag into the ambulance parked behind the newscaster.

"Oh my God!" Angie shrieked.

"I can't believe it," China said flatly, in shock.

Just then, Angie's telephone rang. It was her aunt. She hung up the phone and looked stunned.

"They want me to go identify the body," Angie said. "I don't know if I can do this."

"I'll go with you, if you need someone."

"Yeah. I'd like that."

Angie didn't even blink. She was completely and utterly in shock. The last time they saw Teri, they called her names, even hit her. Now, they'll never get to apologize. She's gone. Gone forever.

When a policeman escorted Teri into the identification room, they made China sit in the waiting area. From down the hall, she could hear Teri screaming: "Oh my God Teri! Teri I'm sorry!"

Then, the same officer brought her back up. She was so distraught that he was helping her walk.

"Angie, let me help you," China said, grabbing one of her arms.

"Ma'am, here's my card," the officer said. "Please give me a call first thing in the morning. We're going to need you to come down to the station and give a statement."

The officer handed her the card.

China got Angie home, but neither of them were in the mood to talk. They sat in the living room and cried their eyes out.

"Teri is gone," Angie cried. "I need to call her mother."

"What are you going to tell the cops?" China asked.

"The truth!" Angie screamed. "I'm going to tell them that Tommy was behind the whole fuckin' thing! He planned it! That's first degree murder!" She was getting hysterical again.

"But Angie," China tried to talk some sense into her, "You don't really know that, do you? You said you heard whispers, but how do you know for sure?"

"Oh, please get off it. We both know what happened. I'm going to police to tell them everything I know. I want this nigga to go down! I'll take him down myself if I fuckin' have to!"

China realized that right when she thought things were settling down, they were just getting crazier than ever.

115

China
Doll

Chapter Nineteen

Goodbye

China ran home and went straight back into her closet. She needed two things, money and firepower.

After collecting exactly what she needed, she gathered a large bag and drove to Angie's place. When she pulled into the driveway, Angie ran out, jumped in the passenger's seat and put her safety belt on."

"Let's bring a mothafucka down." She said.

"Girl, you sound like Foxy Brown."

"Don't I wish," she said with a smile. "Head to the east side. We need to get to Ray Ray.

They headed to the east side, where Angie planned on getting as much information out of Ray Ray as she could. "That motherfucker gon' talk by the time I'm done with 'em," she said.

They pulled up in front of what looked like an abandoned shack.

"Yeah, this is where he lives," she said.

They got out of the car at the same time, both with a "don't fuck with me motherfucker" look on their faces.

China walked up to the front door, taking the left side while Angie took the right. Angie knocked.

"Ray Ray! We need to talk!" A scrawny, 22-year old kid answered the door.

"What up, Angie?"

She shoved past him and walked into the living room.

"Nigga, you got somethin' I want."

"What?"

"Information."

"I ain't squealin' on nobody," he said, "so y'all bitches can just find somewhere else to take that shit.

"I ain't askin' you to squeal, I'm askin' you to save your own life."

"What you mean?" He asked, tilting his head up at Angie, who stood four inches taller than him.

In a quick turn, she stomped on his foot with her stiletto heel. In pain, he winced and doubled over. As soon as he doubled over, she kneed him in the face and he popped back onto the couch, where he lie writhing in pain.

"Damn girl, what the fuck? Where the fuck that come from?"

"Listen," she said, "I'ma ask you this question one time, and I want an answer. I ain't gon hurt you, well, anymore than I already have, but I got shit I need to know."

He looked up at her. "What the fuck is wrong with you?"

"Who killed Teri?"

"Bitch I don't know what the fuck you talkin' about."

Angie took a step toward him and placed her hand on

the back of his neck.

"Listen, lil' nigga. You're gon' tell me what I need to know." She let go of his neck and backhanded him. "Who the fuck killed Teri?

"I don't fuckin' know!" he shouted at her.

BOOM BOOM BOOM.

Angie and Ray Ray both looked at China, who was holding a pistol above her head as chunks of ceiling fell down around her. Smoke was rising from the barrel, fresh after firing the gun to scare both of them into knowing who was running shit.

"I know Angie wants to play nice, but I done had too much shit go down to play nice. I need to know one thing, Ray. Who am I gon' rain down on? Cause I'm pissed, and I'm bringin' someone's house down. It's you, or it's Tommy. I ain't askin' you to squeal on nobody, but I am askin' you one thing. Who should I rain down on?"

He looked at her silently.

"I'm gon' ask you one more time. I had a bad day, and I hate fuckin' repeating myself, but dammit if I'm not feelin' generous today." She walked toward him and put the barrel of the gun against Ray Ray's balls.

"If you ever wanna fuck again, I suggest you tell me the truth. There might even be a little somethin' in it for you. So I'm asking you, one time. Who am I gon' rain down on, you, or Tommy?" His lip started to quiver. "If it's you, say goodbye to your dick. If it's Tommy, tell me where to find him."

A drop of sweat fell from his chin. "If I squeal, he'll kill me!"

"If you tell me where he is, ain't no way he's comin' after you."

His lips were quivering, he looked like he might even piss himself.

"He's with Valerie, over past McNaughton Street."

Angie tapped China.

"I know Valerie. I know exactly where they at, let's

go."

"Wait. One more thing," China said, pausing. She leaned down and grabbed Ray Ray's dick. "If you're lyin' to us, you best say goodbye to your prick, 'cause I'm 'bout to shoot it fulla holes. If we find him, I got ten grand with your name on it."

She pulled a stack of cash from her bag. "Smell it," she said. "You smell 'dat?" He looked her in the eye and nodded.

"He'll be there. He's been fuckin' Valerie for a while now."

"Go figure," China said to Angie. "Whores of a feather flock together. He was fuckin' around on Teri, Teri was fuckin' around on him."

She looked at Ray Ray and rubbed his dick.

"You know, maybe if you play your cards right, I might come back here and fuck the shit outta you on a pile of money."

Ray Ray smiled. "Yeah?"

She slapped him in the face. "Not a chance in hell, pencil dick."

China laughed and walked out.

"Where the fuck did you learn that?" Angie asked.

"Like I said! Foxy Brown!" They got into the car and headed to Valerie's.

Angie pounded on the door. "Val, open up."

They heard muffled voices. "Just a second!"

China shot the doorknob and the door swung open.

"Open sesame," she said. Angie pushed the door open. They saw Tommy standing with wide eyes in the middle of the living room.

"What the fuck are you doing?" He said. "You could've shot me!"

"Shut the fuck up," China said. "Get on your knees."

Tommy put his hands up. "China, I don't understand. What are you doing? What the fuck are you doing?"

China hit him with the butt of her gun. "Shut the fuck

up you piece of shit. Tell me what happened."

"What do you mean what happened? I don't know what the fuck you're talking about!"

"You know damn well what I'm talking about. What the fuck do you know?" China cocked the gun and put it to his forehead. "You best start talkin'."

"Listen, I don't know what you're tryin' to say!"

"China," Angie called from the backyard. She was pointing to two red gas cans by the garbage. "Looks like our boy's been busy."

"Look at that shit!" China called out, nodding toward Angie. "Looks like you're shit outta luck."

"China, listen, it's not what it looks like!" Valerie looked at China. "Whoa, what the fuck is goin' on?"

"Tommy, tell Val what you did."

He started stuttering.

"Nigga!" China kicked him in the stomach with the point of her shoe. "Tell her what the fuck you did!" She pistol whipped him again.

"Val, I don't know what they're talking about!"

"This motherfucker's a little firebug, aren't you? Aren't you Tommy?" China yelled again, kicking Tommy in the gut.

"Yeah, I did it, ok? I fuckin' did it. I burned that bitch's house to the ground, but I didn't know she was there! I didn't know she was home!"

"Well it's too late to deal with excuses. You fucked up, Tommy, you done fucked up."

"I didn't mean to kill her! I swear I didn't mean to kill her! It was an accident!" He paused, "but that fuckin' whore deserved to burn."

"China," Angie called out. "We got what we need?"

"Hell yeah we do." China put her gun away and smirked at Tommy. "Time for us to go."

"Wait," Tommy said. "You're, you're leaving? I don't understand."

"Tommy, you're cute, and from what I hear, you got a

China
Doll

huge dick, but you were always dumb as hell."

China pulled out a small tape recorder from her vest pocket and rewound the tape. Tommy's voice echoed through the silent room. "That fuckin' whore deserved to burn." She pressed the stop button.

Angie, let's go. The boys in blue will wanna hear this. Angie and China turned on their heels and walked out of the apartment, and Tommy didn't say a word.

China got exactly what she wanted, a confession from Tommy. Now, she had one more piece of business to tend to.

China
Doll

PART II

Chapter Twenty

Revenge is the Best Medicine

China's friendship with Angie only grew tighter, especially after they decided to go vigilante all over Baltimore. Something clicked in her that day, something changed. China realized that she was the master of her own destiny, and it was up to her to create the life that she wanted. She'd been through enough at this point, so she was ready to turn it all around.

Months later, Tommy was sitting in jail on ten different charges and Angie had moved past the entire incident. While sitting in her apartment, China decided she needed a change.

She started scouting for apartments all over Baltimore, but she couldn't find anything that she liked. Finally, she met with a realtor who had one final listing for the day. That place, a small one bedroom about thirty minutes from China's current place, was perfect. After making an arrangement to pay for the house completely in cash, China signed the papers and became the proud owner of her first piece of property.

"Angie, I need your help to move to my new place."

Angie squealed in excitement.

"Oh, girl, pick me up in twenty!"

China swung by her place and scooped her, then got on the road.

"Shit, why you movin' so far away?"

"I just need a change of scenery, something' new. Too much has happened in that apartment, too much has happened in Baltimore. Every time someone sees me, they ask 'how are you doing, China?' Sometimes I want to tell them how I really feel, as if they really care. 'Well, my man is in the grave, my own family crossed me, and if Teri were alive, I'd beat that bitch's head into the ground every time I saw her. Oh, yeah, I lost the baby I was carrying too. But, hey, I'm as well as can be expected.'"

China was half joking, but it wasn't funny. Neither of them laughed, instead sitting in silence for a few minutes.

The rest of the afternoon Angie and China packed the rest of China's things and made arrangements for the movers to come the next day. With her millions, China could have opted for a huge house, but she didn't want anyone questioning her status. She didn't know where that money came from, and if it came from somewhere sketch, she didn't want anyone to know she had it. She was staying as low-key as possible.

The townhouse wasn't anything extravagant, but it was nice. It had three floors, huge rooms, an eat-in kitchen, three bathrooms and China's personal favorite, a walk-in closet.

"It's gon' take months to furnish it the way I want,"

she told Angie.

"This shit is hot!" She screamed, her voice echoing off of the empty walls.

"Thanks, girl."

"You must have paid a grip for it."

"Not really, I got a great deal." China was proud of herself. "It was in foreclosure, so I got it for pennies, girl."

"Well let's celebrate," Angie suggested.

"I don't know," China hesitated.

"Come on! We haven't been out since …"

"OK, let's go. My treat."

They decided to drive to DC for dinner because it was only minutes from China's new place.

"Let's hit a club," China suggested.

Her Juicy Couture outfit, Giuseppes and David Yurman jewelry sent the two girls straight to VIP.

"Champagne," China said to the waitress.

"Ooh la la," Angie said, teasing.

China
Doll

They sipped on their bottle of Cristal and danced to the deafening sound of the DJ. China almost forgot about the life she had to go back to after this whole dream was over.

China threw her head back and took a breath. "Girl, this is the life," she said to Angie. When she opened her eyes, a waitress was standing in front of her with another bottle of Cristal.

"From the gentleman across the bar," the waitress said curtly.

"Which man?" China asked. There were at least 20 eyeballing her.

"The one next to the woman in the red dress. He also asked me to give this to you." The waitress handed her a folded paper napkin.

China nodded her head in acknowledgement and unfolded the napkin. "Can't keep my eyes off you. 401-555-9601."

China tried to look at the guy who sent the note, but he was avoiding eye contact.

Angie looked at me with cut eyes. "He's here with some bitch and sendin' you notes? Shady. Who the fuck he think he is?" She said, neck rolling. When she took a second look at him, she realized who, in fact, it was. "Oh, damn girl. I just realized who the fuck that is. It's Sincere."

"Sincere who?"

"I met him a few times with Tommy and Kurt, and not on good terms."

She took another look at Sincere. His lady friend excused herself and walked past the table. Not one second later, Sincere was making his way over.

"I saw you were drinkin' Cristal. I gotta say, sista's got taste."

"We like it," China said like a pro. "But, I'm not so sure your girlfriend would."

"Why do you assume she's my girl?" he asked.

"Why would you wait until she left to come over here if she was just your sister?" China asked, grilling him with confidence. She was too grown for games at this point.

"Listen, call me when you get home. We'll talk about this later." Sincere winked and sauntered away.

China watched his swagger, and she liked it. What she liked even more was that he was a DC boy. A DC boy with connections, and that fed right into China's plan. A plan for revenge. An enemy of Tommy's was a friend of hers. She planned on finding out who shot Jag, the man responsible for starting this whole mess.

"Round one, bring it on," China said under her breath.

Chapter Twenty-One

Sinfully Sincere

"So what's up with Sincere?" China asked Angie as they left the club and headed home.

"I don't know him, personally. Like I said, I just ran into him a few times with Tommy and Kurt a few times. He's big time, China. Not to be fucked with. He's at the top of the DC game, so for some piss-on boys like Kurt and Tommy, there was bad blood. And, something happened once with a buy. Somethin' went wrong once and some niggas ended up getting' shot. I never got the full story. China's thoughts turned to Jag.

That was enough for China. Bad blood is just what she needed for ammunition. If she could get in good with Sincere, things should work out perfectly.

Angie fell asleep on China as they listened to slow jams on the radio on the way home. Shortly, they arrived back at her house.

"You want to spend the night? Your ass is too drunk and too tired to drive back to Baltimore alone."

"I guess," she slurred.

"Here's your bed. You sleep here." China showed her to the guest room, and then kicked off her shoes and stripped out of her clothes. It was close to 5 o'clock in the morning, and her body was exhausted. She slipped into a wife beater and a pair of boy shorts and threw herself into bed. Before her eyes closed, she remembered that Sincere told her to call when she got home. Sleep was beckoning, but it would have to wait. She needed to make that phone call. It was part of her plan.

"Hello," Sincere answered. China heard loud music in the background.

China Doll

"Hey, Sincere, it's China."

"What's up, you home?" he asked. "It's still early."

"Yeah, I just walked in," she yawned.

"I see you follow directions." China rolled her eyes. "That's good, money. Hold on a minute." The noise level went from loud to barely audible.

"Hello?"

"I'm still here. So where's your girlfriend?" she asked.

"Listen, don't worry about that, it's not what you think, but let me know now if you're too insecure to get to know you better. I'd like to think you have as much confidence as you seem to. Being at a club with a chick ain't nothin', but if it's important to you, maybe this phone call was a bad idea," Sincere spit out.

She had to admit, this guy had game, but China had more. She had been dealing with this type for years. Been there, done that. For the sake of what she needed done, she'd play the dumb chick and let him think he was gaming her.

"I'm sorry boo. I didn't mean to come at you like that. I just wanted to make sure that I wasn't steppin' on toes," she lied.

"Let me worry about the toes," he said seductively." So, what's up? What you doin' tomorrow night?" He got straight to the point.

"I was hoping I'd get a chance to see you, that is, if you ain't busy. You seem like a busy man," China said, laying it on thick.

They agreed to meet the next night for dinner and drinks. He told her to pack a bag in case he decided to kidnap her. She planned to do just that. Her mind was moving a million miles a minute. She needed to get her hair, nails and toes done and pick up a few new outfits. Everything needed to be on point.

The next night, she pulled up to the Italian restaurant – something with a name she couldn't pronounce – and checked her makeup and hair one last time before handing the valet her keys. When she entered the restaurant, she spotted Sincere at the bar. She walked over to him and placed a hand on his arm. He looked just as good as she remembered.

131

China
Doll

"Excuse me, are you waiting for someone?" She whispered seductively. He smiled.

"Take a seat. What can I get you to drink?"

"White wine, please,"

"You look nice," he said, eyeing her appreciatively as her took a large gulp of his drink.

"Thanks, I could say the same about you."

Sincere wore an expensive Armani tailored suit, diamond studs in each ear, and his neck and wrist glistened from all the diamonds that adorned them. She was glad she opted for the Cavalli dress that matched perfectly with the Gucci shoes. Together, they looked unstoppable.

China was stunned by how much everything cost. She had been to what she thought were some of the best restaurants, but this was something of a different caliber.

She swallowed hard, regained her composure and ordered the most expensive thing on the menu. Sincere didn't flinch.

Over dinner, he asked her about her life. She told him that she went to Morgan State, worked as a youth counselor and she recently purchased her first home.

"I'm impressed."

Surprisingly, he wasn't the gutter type of dude that China expected. She assumed that he was just another piece of ghetto trash that could speak proper English. Surprise surprise! He was intelligent. This wasn't to say that Jag and Blake weren't intelligent, but they were more street savvy than anything else. She knew that she was dealing with a different breed, now.

"You're beautiful," he said while gazing into her eyes.

"Thank you," she replied, blushing.

"I mean, look at you. You're pretty, your sense of fashion is nothing to be fucked with and you have brains. So tell me, what type of medication are you on?" he asked with a serious look on his face.

"Excuse me?" she said, confused.

"You have to be crazy and on some type of medication. Nobody is this perfect."

They both laughed and continued on with the rest of the night. When they finished dinner, he invited her back to his place for drinks. Naturally, she accepted. She was really enjoying myself, but most importantly, she wanted to get as much information as fast as possible.

When they pulled up to Sincere's apartment building, China was shocked. From the looks of him, you'd think that he lived in a mansion on top of a hill. But instead, he lived in a modest apartment in a high-rise building.

"So, this is it, huh?" she asked, trying not to sound too disappointed.

"No, this is actually just one of my spots. I need to pick up something real quick and then I'll take you to the main house." She knew it!

Sincere grabbed what he came for. "Let's go," he said, heading back to his car. She followed him for another 30 minutes. "Damn, where in the hell are we going?" She asked herself out loud.

They pulled up in front of the most gorgeous houses China had ever seen and got out of their cars.

As they entered the foyer, an older Spanish woman greeted her.

"Buenas noches, señorita."

She nodded her head, then she asked Sincere in a thick Spanish accent if he needed anything.

"No, Marisol, we're fine. I'd like you to meet China. She's a good friend of mine. China, this is my housekeeper, Marisol. We've been together for six years." Sincere smiled at Marisol.

"Nice to meet you, Marisol," she said, smiling. Marisol nodded back.

Sincere led China into the den area. There stood a large bar, Italian leather sofas, and a 62-inch plasma television. The carpet was pure white and thick. Every step she took, she sank inches.

He handed her a glass of wine and they toasted.

"To new friendships."

The night was refreshing. They talked about everything, from art to apartheid. Sincere intrigued her. More than once, she reminded herself that Sincere was only a tool in her pursuit for revenge.

Marisol popped her head in the room. "Señor James, would you like anything before I go to bed?"

"No, it's getting late," he said. She exited the room quietly. China heard her going up the stairs.

"Does she live here?"

"Yes, she's lived with me for three of the six years she's worked for me. I'm not here often, and I need someone to take care of the house. When I am here, I just like to chill and relax. Marisol is a good lady. She's more like a mother to me than anything else." The sun invaded the room through the tiny slits in the blinds.

"It's getting late. We've talked all night long."

"Come here for a minute. I want to show you something," Sincere said.

She followed behind him up the stairs and down a long hallway. He opened two double doors and waved his hand for her to go inside. His bedroom was huge!

"Come with me onto the balcony."

"This is beautiful."

"I come out here sometimes just to watch the sun come up," he said. The sun's orange and red hues lit up the already-stunning view. She didn't know if it was the view, the sun or all the drinks they'd had, but she wanted Sincere.

As if he could read her mind, he walked up behind her and wrapped her in his arms.

"I see something else a little more beautiful."

"You feel good," she whispered, unsure if he could hear her.

China Doll

"Some people take shit like this for granted, but I like to come out here as much as I can. Sometimes I say a prayer and just give thanks for the things I have, sometimes I just like to come out here and clear my head. It's like a world away from all the bullshit that's going on."

"Can I ask you something? You seem to be so different then all of these other guys out here. Why are you still in the business?" She asked, not sure if he would open up so soon.

"China, I've always been different. I've always been the dude who wanted more than just to get by. I started hustling when I was 12. I was tired of being the kid who never had shit. Rundown sneaks, hand-me-down clothes and no real food in the house. My mother worked, but it wasn't nearly enough to give me the things that I wanted. It wasn't really enough to give me the things I needed either. I always had a purpose. Nothing I've done was without a reason. You got these cats out here thinking they big time and wouldn't be able to bail themselves out if it got to that extreme. Dudes get locked up, and their peoples is starving 'cause they weren't smart. That will never be me. I take nothing for granted, and I think about everything I do. If you don't have a plan, you might as well hang it up. I've been doing this for 20 years, and I can account for everything," he said, holding her tighter.

"Will you ever get out?" The question slipped out, though it really didn't matter as far as her revenge went.

"That's the plan," he said, confiding in her.

They stood silently on the balcony until the sun climbed higher.

"You all right?" Sincere asked.

"Yeah, just a little tired, I guess," she lied. It's not the time or the place to unleash the sadness that was trapped inside. Beside, she was just using Sincere. She didn't really care about him. Right?

"Come on." Sincere took her hand and led her into his bedroom.

"Where's your bag?" he asked me.

"Downstairs in my car." He left the room and soon returned with the bag. "You can change in the bathroom."

She stepped into the bathroom and changed into a silk negligee from Victoria's Secret. Then she tied my hair into a loose ponytail and brushed her teeth. Next, the makeup came off, and she applied a thin layer of lip gloss. When she walked back into the bedroom, Sincere was wearing a pair of boxer briefs. His body called to her.

"Damn, maybe I should sleep in the guest room," he joked. She pulled the covers back on the bed and slid in.

"Tired?" he asked.

"Yeah, a little. We've only been up all night long," she laughed.

"Can I hold you?" he said, looking straight into her eyes.

She scooted over toward him with her back to his chest.

"You feel good."

He wrapped his arms around her again and kissed her shoulder. His manhood grew but he never made a move. He lay still, holding her tight until she fell asleep in his arms.

China woke up unsure of where she was. Looking around the room, it took her a minute to realize that she was still at Sincere's place, but he wasn't there. She sat up in bed and realized that he was on the balcony talking on his cell phone. She got out of the bed, although she could have stayed there all day, and walked out to the balcony. His back was turned toward her and he seemed livid.

"Fix it!" he screamed into the phone. China walked over and rubbed his bare back, making her presence known. Sincere took the phone away from his ear and kissed her softly on the lips.

China
Doll

"Are you hungry?" he asked.

She nodded my head. "Starving."

He kissed her again and put up his index finger motioning for her to wait. "Give me a minute."

China walked back into the bedroom, pulled her robe out of her bag and waited. Soon, Sincere ended his call and came into the bedroom.

"I'm sorry about that. You leave a boy to do a man's job and shit is bound to get fucked up," he said.

"Should I go so you can handle your business?"

Sincere removed her robe. He kissed her neck and slipped each strap of her nightgown off her shoulders. Her negligee dropped to the floor, and she stood naked in front of him. Sincere stared at her body and led her back to the bed. A part of her wanted to stop him. China didn't want things to move too fast, but she couldn't resist. There was something about him that was drawing her in, something that made her want to be close to him. In this one moment, the need to feel love overpowered any need for anything else. China smiled.

He laid her on her back and started kissing her feet. He sucked on each toe, moved up to her ankles, slowly kissed her calves, the back of my knees, my thighs, and after many tender kisses, he finished at my cherry spot. The sun, the moon and the stars all exploded before her eyes.

"Sincere, please stop," China begged.

"You don't want me to stop, baby."

She laughed. "You're right. I don't want you to stop." She held on to his head and pushed his face deeper. Within minutes, she reached a third, then fourth climax.

"You like that?" Sincere asked. He released his grip and sat up. Next, he kissed her stomach and fondled her breasts.

"Come here," she said, wanting to feel all of him.

"Come on, let's eat," he said, laughing.

"Eat?" China asked him, confused. "I'm not hungry for food," she said, touching his chest.

"I am." Sincere stood up and pulled her off the bed.

Hesitantly, she threw on my negligee and followed him down to the kitchen, dripping wet between the legs.

"Take what you want," he said while drinking a glass of orange juice. "Muffins, Danish, orange juice, fruit and bagels." His eyes didn't leave hers. "Marisol didn't know what time we were getting up. Usually, she prepares a hot breakfast," he said.

"It's perfect," China said, grabbing a muffin and then a glass of juice.

Sincere sat across from where China was standing. Her body was still trembling from their short escapade upstairs. She walked over to him and placed her food on the table, then she straddled him.

"Can I have some now?" she asked.

He laughed. "Do you see something you like?"

She slid his manhood out of his boxer briefs, raised her nightgown and mounted him. Her hips rotated slowly, and she never lost eye contact with him. After a moment, she teased him by stopping.

"No, I don't think so." He palmed her ass and moved her back and forth, and then a soft moan slipped from his throat.

"I'm coming," she whispered in Sincere's ear. Then she heard the clicking of high-heeled shoes. "I think Marisol is coming," she said in a whisper.

"Keep going," he insisted, holding onto me tightly.

China tried to stop. "Sincere —"

"Shhhhh," he said, "Keep going."

With each thrust, the clicking of shoes grew louder. She knew that Marisol would be coming into the kitchen any second. Even though she didn't want to be caught in the act, she couldn't stop either. Knowing they were about to get caught excited her even more.

Marisol entered the kitchen and caught her riding the hell out of Sincere. "Sincere …" she said again. He wouldn't let her go. "Oh, baby, you feel so good."

"Sincere, we have company," she whispered as he continued to move inside of her.

He didn't stop. "Oh, this pussy is good. Fuck, yeah, it feels so good."

"Sincere!" she yelled, snapping him out of his trance. Was this something normal, for Marisol to see her boss fucking women at the breakfast bar surrounded by muffins and bagels?

Sincere looked at her and then at Marisol. He still hadn't stopped fucking her.

"Marisol, wanna give us a minute?" he asked.

"Yes sir," she responded and walked out.

Sincere picked China up and shoved her back against the wall. Then he rammed the hell out of her. "Oh, bitch, you like this dick? Uh, uh, take this dick, bitch," he grunted in her face.

She held onto his neck. "Daddy, fuck me, Daddy!" She screamed back.

Sincere pumped faster and harder. His sweat flew all

China
Doll

over. He bit down on her shoulder. "It feels so good," he moaned.

Then he carried her to the living room and put her on the couch. There he hiked one of her legs over the back of the sofa and draped the other over his shoulder. "You like this, baby?"

"Work it, Daddy," she gasped. He did.

Their bodies jerked and twitched at the same time. They were drenched in each other's fluids. She slid, he slid, they moaned and erotic noises filled the quiet room.

"Sincere …" she sighed.

"Boom, boom, boom," he whimpered as he left a puddle of babies swimming on her stomach.

They lay side-by-side, stomachs rising and falling with each labored breath. Sincere brushed her hair back with his large fingers.

"Do you always have sex in front of your housekeeper?" she asked, still breathing hard.

"No, but she knows not to question anything that I do. Her job is to maintain the upkeep of my house and prepare my meals. I don't pay her enough to comment on anything else. Did it make you uncomfortable?"

"Yeah, a little," she admitted.

They spent the rest of the day locked in his bedroom exploring each other's bodies. China was exhausted, but she couldn't get enough of him. Before they knew it, three days had passed.

"Listen, I have to make a run. Do you mind waiting for me here until I come back?" he asked.

"Do you want me to? I've taken up a lot of your time over the past few days. Maybe I should go home and let you get back to business," she said seriously. She hadn't been home in days, and her cell phone had been turned off since the first night she spent with Sincere. She needed to get back to reality.

"I won't be gone long. Just chill for a minute and make yourself at home." Sincere kissed her on my lips and walked out of the bedroom.

When she heard the door shut she ran a hot bath. Her body ached as if she'd endured a strenuous workout. While the water ran, she pinned my hair up and took a BCBG sweat suit out of her bag and lay it across the bed. The water felt so good. She closed my eyes and thought about the past few days.

She just had to keep reminding herself that she was not interested in falling in love. This is all about revenge, not feelings "Señor James asked me to assist you in whatever you need."

Marisol scared China, and she nearly jumped across the room. Water splashed all over the floor.

"What are you doing in here?" China yelled.

"Señor James asked me to assist you," she repeated.

"I don't need any assistance, so can you please get the fuck out of the bathroom?!" She screamed, trying to cover herself with the little washcloth. This lady is nuts. She stood in the doorway of the bathroom, hands folded and not budging.

China
Doll

"I'll be damned if you're going to watch me in this damn tub," China screamed at her.

Quickly, she jumped out of the tub and wrapped a towel around her wet body. "Listen, I'm not sure how you normally interact with Sincere's friends, but I do not need any assistance. If you will excuse me, I would like to get back to my bath in privacy."

"Yes, ma'am," Marisol nodded and left the bathroom. She slammed the door shut and locked it. "Thank you," China muttered to myself.

After two hours alone in the big house, China was bored senseless so she checked her voicemail. There were six messages from Angie.

"Hello," Angie answered.

"Hey, girl, what's up?" China asked.

"Girl, where have you been? I have been calling you for days!" she yelled into the phone.

She laughed out loud. "I'm still at Sincere's house. Sorry I didn't call, but we've been a little busy. He's out now, so I figured I'd check my messages."

"You could have called me, China! I've been worried. So what's up with Sincere anyway? The least you can do is give me the details!" she said, now laughing.

China ran down dinner, how beautiful his house is, and how weird Marisol is. She left out the sex. The last time China bragged about that, she had to beat a pregnant bitch down. "If I'm not coming home tonight I'll call you to let you know."

After they hung up, China walked downstairs into the kitchen. "I should make this nigga one of my special dinners. He's treated me, so I'll treat him."

She got out the pots and pans, and immediately, Marisol came running into the kitchen.

"El qué demonios!" she yelled.

"English," China stated coldly. "Is there a problem?"

"I cook for Señor James," Marisol scowled.

"Listen, why don't you take the rest of the day off, because honestly, I'm tired of looking at you. I'll be the one cooking for Sincere tonight."

Marisol stomped out of the kitchen and walked back upstairs.

"That bitch is starting to get on my nerves," China said under her breath. She made steaks with mashed potatoes and homemade gravy, collard greens, macaroni and cheese and two sweet potato pies. She really outdid herself.

Sincere walked into the kitchen. "Hey," he said looking into each pot and dish.

"Hey, back at you. Everything straight?" she asked.

"Yeah, what got into Marisol? She made enough food to feed an army."

"Actually, I cooked. I figured you'd be hungry when you got back, so I wanted to make you something special. Sorry, I got a little carried away." Sincere looked at her with raised brows.

"You cooked this?"

"Yeah," she smiled at him, proud of what she'd done.

Again he examined the food.

"Am I going to die after I eat this?" he joked.

China threw the dishtowel at him and started to fix his plate. "Go sit down and I'll bring you your food."

"A nigga can get used to this."

"We'll see about that, " she laughed.

After seconds and thirds, Sincere couldn't stop talking about her cooking.

"Where did you learn to cook like that? I haven't eaten like this since my mother was alive."

"The South, baby. Every Southern girl can burn."

China
Doll

Chapter Twenty-Two

Ride with Me

After spending a week with Sincere, China finally broke away and came back home. Compared to his house, her house looked like a shack – but it was her house. As soon as she kicked off her shoes, the doorbell rang.

"What's up, Angie?" she said, pulling the door open.

"Hey, long time no see, girl," she said, stepping around her to get in the door.

"Yeah, it's been a long week. Sincere is cool, though," China said, smiling.

"He must be for you to be MIA for a week straight. Hey, I got some info on your boy," she announced.

"Sincere?"

"Yup. I ran into Poppo the other day, and he asked

about you. I was telling him that you're holding up. He started saying how sorry he was that you've been through so much. First Jag, then the baby, then Blake. Poppo must have been drinking 'cause then he started running off at the mouth. Talking about how those DC boys is still doing everybody dirty. He said they just ran up on Skeelo and Jaz the other night."

"What does that have to do with Sincere?"

"Poppo said these dudes work for Sincere."

China was dumbfounded. "So, are you telling me that Sincere is responsible for killing Jag?" she jumped up. "What the fuck?"

This news made her even more anxious to move on the plan. So, Sincere may have had something to do with these other deaths. China was a bitch on a mission right now. Her shit needed to be tight. She was dealing with some ruthless niggas, and they wouldn't think twice about erasing a glitch in their plots.

"That's what Poppo said. Sincere is running shit, so nothing goes down without his say-so. And word is that Tommy was trying to set up Kurt and Blake. He was trying to be down with Sincere."

This was way too much to digest. Sincere had something to do with Jag being shot. He was down with Tommy, which means if he still speaks to Tommy and China's name should come up, she could be a dead bitch. She had no idea what to do next.

"You all right?" Angie asked, snapping her out of her thoughts.

"Yeah, I mean, I guess so. I just can't believe I spent a week with the man who killed Jag. And if he's cool with Kurt, and he finds out that I'm the one who testified against him, he could kill my ass, too."

"China, I doubt you have anything to worry about. Tommy wasn't on his team; he was only trying to be. He wasn't making money for Sincere, so I can't see how you would be affected," Angie assured her.

"I snitched on Tommy," China said. "I sat in that courtroom and testified. Who knows what real ties he has with Sincere."

Days passed, and China had to ignore hundreds of Sincere's phone calls. She was happy that he didn't know where she lived because judging from the voicemails, he'd come looking for her. One night at three in the morning my phone rang. "Hello?" she answered.

Fuck, she didn't check the caller ID.

"Are you ignoring me?" Sincere asked.

"What?" China said, still a little groggy.

"Why aren't you answering my calls?" he asked again.

"Sincere, it's three o'clock in the morning. Can we talk about this later?" she asked, pissed at herself for being so careless.

"We could have talked about it 4 days ago, but you haven't returned my calls. Look, if I'm playing myself, let me know," he stated coldly.

"I've just been busy, please don't take it personal. You held me captive for a week, remember? I had a few things I needed to take care of," she lied.

"Listen, I need to handle some business of my own. I'm going out of town for a few days. I should be back on Friday. When I get back, I want to see you. Do you think you'll have all your loose ends tied by then?"

"Yeah, yeah, call me when you get back."

"Listen, anything you got going on now is cool. But end it before I get back." Sincere hung up.

Friday came with no call from Sincere – China wasn't tripping, though. She wanted to get a few things done, mainly shopping. She hit up Nordstrom, Saks, and did a little online shopping for shoes. By the time she satisfied her shopping appetite, she had spent more than $10,000. But, after all, the temperature was dropping and she needed new fall clothes.

It was Sunday, and still no word from Sincere. Now

she was mad. More like pissed. Could this be her payback for not returning his calls? Shit, she wasn't having it. After debating for ten minutes, she decided to call him.

"Hello," he answered.

"Hey, it's China," she said, somewhat annoyed.

"What's up?" he asked, as if they spoke just yesterday.

"Just checking on you. I thought I would've heard from you, uh, on Friday, like you said."

"Yeah, I thought I'd give you a few more days to handle your business. Everything straight now? I don't have to worry about you dipping off on me no more, do I?"

"I'm cool," she said. Did he just check her?

"Good. I want to see you. Is that cool? I want to come by and check you out."

Think of a lie, think of a lie. "Um, actually, my place is still a mess from when I moved in. They're still laying down my floors and most of my shit is still in boxes."

"All right, all right, then why don't you meet me at my house? I should be home in a few hours. I'll have Marisol let you in. Make yourself at home, and I'll see you there."

"OK, I'll leave in a few."

"China, I really missed you," he said before hanging up.

Again she packed a bag. This time, she packed for a month. She didn't want to run out of clothes. Not that she had clothes on that often. This time, she planned to bring some things to keep her busy if Sincere had to leave her in his house again. Within the hour, she was flying down the highway toward Sincere's place.

China pulled into the driveway. "Thank God that nigga is here," she said, seeing Sincere's car parked in front of the house. She didn't want to be stuck in that house with Marisol. China pulled her bag out of the trunk and rolled it up to the front door, then rang the doorbell once.

Marisol answered. "Is Señor James expecting you?"

China Doll

she asked, blocking the doorway.

"What do you think?" she replied with attitude, walking right past her.

Sincere greeted her in the living room with a sloppy kiss. "I see you brought enough this time," he said, looking at the bag. He smacked China on my ass.

She laughed. "Can I get a little help taking my things upstairs?"

"You need me to help you, huh? What can I help you with?" he teased.

"Let me show you," she said, smiling seductively.

They walked into his bedroom, and she pulled off her shirt and unsnapped her bra. "Do you remember these?" she asked, shaking her breasts in his face.

"Hell, yeah. I missed these motherfuckers, too." He kissed all over her breasts, then pushed them together and buried his face between them. After playing with them, he picked her up and placed her gently on the bed, then he tugged at her jeans. Finally, he just ripped them off.

"Hey, man, what are you doing?"

"I'll buy you another pair, baby. I'll buy you a hundred pairs of them." He threw them on the floor.

"No panties! Hell, no. Bitch, come here. I got some shit for you right here."

He inserted two fingers inside her.

"Oh God!" she screamed out, "Sincere, baby, oh, you're hitting my g-spot!"

Over and over again he hit the spot. She didn't want to come yet, but she didn't think she could stop it. She breathed her hot breath on his neck. "I'm loving it, Daddy. You're so fucking good."

Sincere didn't ease up. He sat up and unbuckled his pants, letting them drop to the floor. "You want some of this dick?"

He stepped out of his boxer briefs and turned China onto her stomach. "Call my name, bitch." Sincere entered her from behind and grabbed onto her breasts.

147

China
Doll

"Sincere, baby, you make me feel so good," she called out.

He pushed himself as deep inside her as he could go.

"Say it, bitch! Say my name!"

"Oh, Sincere! Fuck me, Daddy!" she hollered as loud as she could, hoping that bitch, Marisol, could hear that raunchy, nasty-ass fucking.

Sincere's hand found its way down to her clit. "Oh, fuck!" she moaned.

He flicked it until she created a puddle all over his sheets.

"Ride me," he commanded. "Climb the fuck up on me, bitch."

She climbed on top of him, easing herself down and started off slow. "You feel that, Daddy?" she asked him.

She stared at him and put her finger in her mouth. She pretended her finger was his dick. She ran her hand through her hair and rose and fell on his hard cock. He didn't say a word because his eyes had rolled up into his head. She was pretty sure he was good to go, so she picked up my pace.

China
Doll

"Open your eyes, Daddy," she told him. Then she grabbed her breasts and began to lick at her nipples. Slowly, she began to fondle them one by one.

"Wait, wait, slow down. I don't want to come yet," he said grabbing her hips. Sincere flipped her over and jumped on top of her, pumping inside of her with force. "Take this, bitch!" he growled.

She wrapped her legs around his waist and held on tight. He pulled her hair while he dug into her. "I love it," she screamed.

It had been forever since she'd had sex like this. She wasn't sure if she would be able to walk after this episode. They were sweating so much you'd think they were in a sauna. Secretly, she wished they had a video camera. This was surely worth some dollars.

Suddenly, Sincere stopped, got off the bed and pulled

her to the edge. There he entered her again from behind, all the while grunting and making noises she'd never heard come from a human before. China was fucking turned on. God, she wished this could go on forever.

She flipped over again and put both of her feet over his right shoulder. "Oh my God!" She instantly came. This went on for 20 more minutes.

"Boom, boom, boom," Sincere said as he released everything inside of her.

"Oh, Daddy, you beat my kitty the hell up."

"But did it feel good?" he looked at her. He was all sweaty.

"It hurt so good!" she smiled.

"Tell me something about you," Sincere said as he stroked her hair. She could smell herself all over him.

"I've told you everything," she answered. She could barely catch her breath.

"I'm sure there's more to you than a college degree, work and a new house."

"What do you want to know?" she asked.

"Tell me why you're single. Tell me why someone hasn't married you and why don't you have beautiful children that look just like you."

Her body became rigid. She tried hard to fight back the tears, but she couldn't. She was about to lose it, and there was no stopping it. Before she could open her mouth to speak, tears streamed down her face.

"What's wrong? Did I say something wrong?" Sincere asked.

She couldn't speak. All she did was cry. She thought about her engagement to Jag, the night he died, and how Blake killed himself right in front of her. She thought about all that she had lost and how it seems that she will never be able to hold onto anything. It seemed as if everyone he ever truly loved was taken from her. She felt empty inside. Sincere was quiet. He wrapped his arms around her and let her cry.

149

China Doll

She cried all that night until morning. Her eyes were bloodshot and puffy. Her voice was hoarse. Sincere never left her side.

"What happened to you?" he gently asked.

"A whole lot."

"Tell me," he said, still holding her.

She wanted to tell him everything. She wanted to rid herself of these memories and thoughts instead of keeping them bottled inside. But how could she? How could she share this information with the man who had something to do with her pain? She was supposed to be here to seek revenge, but she was getting caught up against her better judgment. She hated herself more now for entertaining the thought of catching feelings for this man. How could she enjoy herself so much with him? And why does he have to be so damn sweet all the time?

"Sincere, I really can't talk about it right now, OK? Just give me some time," she said, wiping the tears with a tissue.

"Fair enough. Then I'll tell you about me." He sat up in bed. "I grew up in PG County with my mother. My father died when I was 11, and my mother never brought another man in the house after that. She worked two, three, sometimes four jobs to make sure I had enough. It was never enough, but she tried. I couldn't take coming home and the lights were cut off or going to bed hungry 'cause dinner wasn't enough to fill my stomach. I was tired of being teased at school because my tennis shoes were raggedy and my clothes didn't fit me right. So I started hanging with some old heads around the way, and I started hustling. By the time I was 17, I was doing my thing. I had cars, my own apartment, and enough money to take care of my mother. She knew where the money was coming from and didn't like it, but she never turned it away. Twenty years later, here I am, big house, nice cars, jewelry, clothes and no one to share it with. My mother has always been the closest person in my life, but I lost

China
Doll

her a few years back. I told myself that I wouldn't get close to anyone after that; that kind of loss was too hard. I said I'd keep these women at arm's length because loving someone wasn't worth it when you lose them in the end."

She looked up at Sincere, and he was wiping tears from his eyes. I guess thugs cry, too. He was right about one thing — it doesn't pay to fall in love. Without warning, everything important to you can be taken away. Then what do you have? Not a fucking thing. She tried love, even after Jag, and look where it got her.

"Let's go out." Sincere suggested. "I want to cheer you up. We can go wherever you want to go." He smiled tenderly.

China smiled back.

ω ω ω ω ω ω ω ω ω ω ω ω ω ω ω ω ω

151

*China
Doll*

They walked into the roller skating rink.

"I can't believe that I let you talk me into this."

"You said anywhere," China laughed.

They exchanged their shoes for skates and sat down on one of the benches to put them on. The DJ was playing some old-school skate music. She was instantly taken back. Teri, Angie and China used to go to the skating rink every weekend during their sophomore year.

"I cannot believe you got me out here on skates. I thought you'd ask me for dinner and a movie — shit, even shopping — but skating? I'm just going to watch you from here," Sincere said, holding onto the wall.

"No, you're coming out here and skate with me," she laughed. China grabbed his hand and dragged him out to the rink. Planet Rock was playing. Now, she was feeling it.

Sincere rolled out onto the skating floor and fell flat on his ass.

"Oh my God!" she laughed. "Come on, baby. Let me

help you back up."

He held tightly onto her hand, and they awkwardly moved around the rink.

"Where's the suave man from last night?" she asked laughing.

After 20 minutes of struggling and falling, Sincere convinced her to let him watch from outside the rink. She flew around the rink about a dozen times, pearling and bouncing to the music. She really was having a good time, but wished that Sincere was out there with her.

"I'm ready to go."

"I can't believe you let me get out there and embarrass myself like that," he laughed, changing his shoes.

"What black person can't skate?"

"Me!"

They both burst out laughing. Man, did she need a laugh. Then they walked through the parking lot holding hands.

152

China Doll

After some thought, she decided to pack her things and go home. This situation was starting to get too intense. She needed to distance herself before she ended up somewhere that she had no intention of being.

"Sincere, I'm going to head home. I need to clear my head a little bit. I'll call you when I get there," she said as he stuffed her belongings in a bag. "Look, we're not together, this isn't a relationship, so you can do what you please. I think we could use a little time apart to get our heads together and be more realistic about this situation."

She continued to throw her clothes into her bag, and then looked around the room to see if she had forgotten anything.

"Honestly, Sincere, I don't even know you. I met you in a club while you were with someone else. I spent a few days in your house, and yeah, we were intimate, but that doesn't mean that this is a relationship." She stopped and looked at him. "Yeah, you're a very nice person, and I like you, but I'm not trying to rush into anything. I hope you agree."

"Yo, you can do what you need to do. Clear your head, take a couple of days, that's fine. But what you really need to do is be real with yourself. You can play games day in and day out. I could care less. But the sooner you start admitting that you like what's going on between us and that you do care, the easier it will be. Why'd you call me, China? The first phone call, coming to my house on a whim and staying for a week. Packing a bag to stay again. Why do all of this for someone you're not feeling?" He stood up. "I won't push you to do anything. I'll give you all the space you need. I can do that. I pride myself on shutting bitches out. So when you feel like you're ready to stop playing these stupid-ass games, holla at me. If I ain't too busy, I might invite you over."

She was speechless. She looked at him and wondered if she made a mistake.

The entire ride she cursed herself. She hated the fact that she let him get to her. She hated that what she really wanted to do was turn the car around and go back to his house.

China
Doll

"Fuck this," she said. She made a U-turn and headed straight back to his house. She had to play her part. If she wanted revenge, she had to keep him close, right? This had nothing to do with how she felt about him. She was just doing what she had to do to make sure things go the way she wanted them to go.

China pulled up in Sincere's driveway, and his car was there. He must have pulled off just to let off some steam. She got her bag out of my car and rang the doorbell.

Sincere answered. "Yeah?" he said coldly.

"Can I come in?"

He stepped aside to allow her to come in. Reaching down, he took her bag and went upstairs with it. A moment later, he returned and walked into the living room. She followed behind him to try to clear the air. She couldn't afford to have him cut her off just yet.

"Sincere, can we talk?"

"What's up? All I need to hear from you is I'm sorry."

She was quiet. It took all she had in herself to keep quiet. She wanted to blast him in his face. Who the hell does he think he's fucking with? Instead, she inhaled deeply.

"I'm sorry," she said quietly.

He stared at her. She couldn't tell if he was undressing her with his eyes or if he was devising a plan to kill her and bury her in the basement. She knew he was capable of disaster. "I'm not to be fucked with."

"Look, I've gone through a lot in my life. Some horrible things have happened to me and getting close to people isn't easy for me to do, either. I'm sure you can understand that. It's easier for me to walk away. I'm sorry if I upset you, because I didn't mean to. I don't know what your motives are, and I don't know you. How can I trust that you're being honest about how you feel?"

She should have won an Oscar for her performance. That or someone to smack her in my face and make her realize she cannot fall for this man. She was scaring herself.

"China, I have friends, and I have women that I fuck. I have women who I fuck who don't know how to let go and move on. I'm very honest with the people I deal with. If I don't want more than a one-night stand, you will be well aware of that from the door. Although I'm not big on letting people inside my world, I'm real big on accepting my feelings when I have them. Damn it, I like you, China, and I want to get to know you. But I'm not forcing you to give in to that. The choice is yours."

Wow! She should be shooting this man's brains clear out of his head, but instead, she wanted to run to him, hide in his love and never look back. Talk about betrayal.

She spent another week at Sincere's smoothing things over. By the time she packed her things to leave, she had

154

China
Doll

him wrapped around her little finger. Sadly, she was just as sprung. She promised to let him visit her house the following week so they could spend a few days together there.

"What am I thinking? For some reason, I can't tell his ass no — especially when all nine and a half inches of him are deep inside of me. What is a girl to do?" she thought to herself.

She got home and decided to clean her house and do some laundry. Cleaning always helps her think clearly. She needed to come up with a way to limit her feelings for Sincere.

She called Angie. "What's up? Let's go out tonight."

"Oh, so now you want to hang out with me?" Angie yelled in the phone. "I shouldn't go nowhere with you. You start hanging with Sincere and ain't got no time for nobody."

"Come on, Ange, let's go out. We can find some new friends and bring them back to my house. You know you need a friend!" she sang.

"Yeah, 'cause you know I ain't been ridden in a minute. All right, all right, I'll be at your house at 11."

After a long hot shower, searching her closet for something to wear and a long beauty regime, they finally headed to a club. As soon as they stepped inside, they walked straight to the bar.

"I need a drink," China said. She ordered a shot of vodka.

"What do you want, Angie?"

"Get me a Kamikaze."

"Are you trying to walk out of here tonight, or am I going to have to carry your ass?"

"Somebody is going to carry my ass. I'm ready to get fucked up."

The men started to flock to them. They didn't have to pay for any more drinks.

"Excuse me, did you go to Morgan State?"

China
Doll

"Yes," China answered. She couldn't stop looking at his beautiful mouth.

"I think we were in the same child psychology class. Your name is China, right?" he asked.

"Yeah, you look familiar to me, too. I'm sorry, I don't remember your name."

"I'm Marc Lewis." He held out his hand. "Can I buy you a drink?"

She shook his hand.

"I'll take a shot of vodka and a Sex on the Beach."

"Wow, sounds like you're trying to get drunk tonight."

"Just a little."

Marc and China made small talk for a while.

"You want to go to the VIP?"

"Of course," she said.

She tapped Angie on her shoulder. "I'll be right back."

*China
Doll*

China followed Marc to the second level. He told her that he lives about 20 minutes from her neighborhood, and he works at a mental hospital counseling patients. She didn't really remember him from school, but was glad he approached her anyway. He had a fresh cut, manicured nails, smooth skin and nice body. He was definitely her type.

"Listen, I gotta get going. I have an early morning tomorrow. Is it OK if I call you sometime?" he asked, getting up from his seat.

"Sure." she recited her number while Marc programmed it into his cell phone.

"I'll call you soon." He kissed her on the cheek.

She couldn't stop smiling. Finally she met a regular nigga. A nice guy with a normal job.

Angie was seated at a table with two men. She smiled at China.

"Hey, girl, this is Tony and his friend Zion."

She smiled at the two men and took a seat next to Zion.

He was cute but not her type. He was a lot shorter than she liked her men, and his hair was braided. She hated braids — especially on grown men.

Angie invited the two men back to China's house. Five minutes after they walked through the door, she and Tony disappeared.

"You have a nice place. Do you live here alone?" Zion asked, looking around.

"Yeah, just me," she answered.

"Do you have anything to drink?" China went to the kitchen, grabbed a beer and handed it to him with a coaster. Then she sat down next to him and looked around the room trying to think of something to talk about. They had no chemistry. She could think of a million other places she'd rather be. She also hoped this nigga wouldn't try to make any moves. China and Zion could hear Angie in the other room moaning as if she was getting served more dick than she's had in a while. "He better not be getting horny," China thought.

Zion placed his hand on her thigh, leaned over and tried to whisper in her ear as he placed his other hand on her breast.

"Nigga you crazy?" she asked, jumping up.

"Come on, baby. Let me make you feel good. I know you feel it."

"I guess you think just because my girl is giving it up in the next room I should be doing the same."

"Damn, girl, you look so good."

"Are you hearing me?"

Zion grabbed her and thrust his tongue down her throat. Then he grabbed her hair, pulled her head back forcefully and nibbled on her neck. Oh, hell, no!

"Listen, I got a man, and he ain't a low life like you. Take the weak shit somewhere else." He looked stunned.

"Come on girl, let me get some," he said.

"Get some? Nigga please. I'm going to bed. I want you gone by the time I wake up in the morning." She stood up, walked to her room and buried her head in the pillow.

China's cell phone rang and woke her up. She looked at the caller ID. It was Sincere at six o'clock a.m.

"Hello?"

"Hey, sorry to wake you, baby, but I can't sleep."

"What's wrong? Did something happen?"

"Business," Sincere replied.

"Do you want to talk about it?"

"I want to see you. I'm on my way to your house."

"Now?" Her stomach suddenly started doing flips. How could she get these people out of her house? She panicked.

"I should be there in about an hour. I got to handle something real quick, then we can talk when I get there. So get rid of that nigga." Sincere hung up before she could ask him what he meant.

How in the hell does he know people are here? She rushed to the guest bedroom.

China Doll

"Angie, open up the damn door." China pounded on the door. She pulled the door open, a sheet wrapped around her body. "What's up?" she asked, rubbing her eyes.

"Them niggas have to go. Tony and Zion have to go," she whispered, urgently. "Sincere just called, and he's on his way over here."

"Why does Tony have to go?" she whined.

"Come on. Come on, Angie. Because Sincere doesn't need to think that I'm running a fucking hotel. Get his ass up and out of here. I'll take care of Zion."

"Zion! Get your ass up!" He grabbed China and pulled her onto the couch.

"Fucking stop it, Zion. Get up, you got to go."

"All right, give me a few more minutes. It's still early, girl," he said, turning his back toward me.

"No! Get up, now! The party's over."

"Damn, girl." With a frown, he got out of bed and started putting his clothes on.

"Bye, Zion." Tony was already waiting, talking to

Angie.

"Kiss him and bring your ass back in here," China shouted to her.

A moment later, Angie came barreling back into the house. "What's going on?"

"I told you, Sincere is on his way. Speaking of which, he has some things he wants to talk about so I'm going to need you to head out, too. He sounded like something serious is going down. I'll call you later."

She didn't give Angie a chance to protest.

After her shower, China put on sweatpants and a wife beater, threw her hair into a messy ponytail and ran through the house straightening up. She hadn't done anything wrong, but inviting men over to your house in the middle of the night isn't something any man wants to see. She heard a car pull into the driveway.

The doorbell rang.

"What's up?" Sincere said as he walked into her house.

"Hey, you OK?" she asked, genuinely concerned.

"Are we alone?" he asked, looking around.

"Yeah, Angie was here, but I sent her home."

"Nice place. You want to show me around?"

She showed Sincere through the house and then they cuddled up on the couch. She could tell that whatever was bothering him was something serious. He had the same look on his face that Blake used to have when something went wrong. She knew that his desire to hurt something or someone was as good as done.

"Talk to me," China said, stroking his head.

"Some of my peoples were supposed to make a pickup for me today, and they got robbed. I'm talking over fifty grand. Somebody gotta pay for this."

From past experience, she knew not to dig too deeply. She didn't ask any questions, just listened and read between the lines of what he was talking about. Sincere thought China wasn't familiar with the street life, but she knew

159

China
Doll

exactly what he was talking about. She knew exactly what was going to go down.

"Did you have fun last night?" he asked out of the blue.

"What?" She asked, trying to play ignorant.

"You went out, right? Did you have fun?" he asked again, looking directly into her eyes.

"Yeah, it was all right. Me and Angie had our ladies' night," she replied with a smile, trying to read him.

"You ain't done playing games yet, I see," he said.

"What are you talking about? If you have something to say to me, why don't you just come out and say it."

"Yeah, that's what I thought. You ain't ready yet. Look, I'm going to have to cancel this week. I got to take care of some business."

She pouted.

"All right."

"You mad?" he asked me.

"Just a little disappointed."

"Just ride with me on this, all right, China? I'll make it up to you. Just stay out of the clubs and keep them niggas out yo' crib."

That convinced her that Sincere either has a GPS tracking device or he's having her watched.

"Excuse me?" She asked.

"Look, I'll let you live for now," he smiled at her, "but you need to air yourself out. I'll be back in a week, all right?"

Still pouting, she said, "All right."

He kissed her on my forehead and got up to leave.

She realized that the unexpected trip to her house wasn't about him wanting to talk; it was to check up on her. He's obviously checking her respect level. She wondered where she weighed on the scale.

For days she wandered around her house, keeping herself busy. She missed Sincere, and there was no denying it. The week he was supposed to be gone turned into three weeks, and he stopped answering her calls. Gone for almost a month and not even a phone call? She was way past stressed. Over the weeks, though, she avoided the clubs and all of Marc's calls. She knew Sincere wasn't the kind of nigga to be fucked with, so she kept it cool.

Angie called one night, all stressed about a guy she was talking to, so she turned her phone off and had a few drinks too many. When she left Angie's house the next morning, she got into her car and turned on her cell phone, checking her messages. Three were there from Sincere asking where she was and why her phone was off. Go figure. He's MIA for damn near a month, and his ass calls as soon as she decided to venture out. Taking a deep breath and gathering her thoughts, China dialed Sincere's number.

"Hello."

"Hey, I just saw that you called me last night." "Why was your phone off?" he asked. "I turned it off," China replied sarcastically.

China
Doll

"Where are you? I've been sitting outside your house since two o'clock in the morning."

"I spent the night with Angie. She's going through it over some guy she's seeing. I didn't feel like driving home in the middle of the night."

She continued my conversation with him until she reached her house. When she pulled up, there he was, leaning on the hood of his car.

"Hey," she said, standing on my tiptoes to give him a kiss.

"We need to talk," he said, walking toward my house.

"Sure." she unlocked her door, and we entered.

"What's up with you? First, it starts with you not answering my calls, now you're spending the night out and running the streets. What's going on?"

"Excuse me? Maybe we both need to clarify a few things. Let's start by establishing what this is. Are you my man, Sincere? Are we in a committed relationship? The last thing you said when you left was that you'd be gone for about a week. Well, it's been closer to a month since I've heard from you. I've called and left messages, and you never called me back. What do you want me to do? You're asking so much from me, but what are you giving me in return? And for the record, all this possessive shit is real corny. 'Where you at? What are you doing? Why didn't you answer the phone?' You cannot be serious."

Sincere looked at me. "Look, I need someone to ride with me right now. Can you handle that? I don't need to deal with someone I can't trust, especially with the position I'm in. Whether I'm gone for six days or six months, I need to know that you're home waiting on me. If you can't handle that, let me know now. I knew you were the type of woman I wanted when I first met you, but now I'm getting second thoughts."

162

China Doll

"You still talking like I owe you something. Yeah, we kicked it for a few months, but so what? I'm sure you've done it bigger than this with plenty of other women. If I'm riding with you, I need to have some type of knowledge about what I'm riding with; who I'm riding with. Secrets are now out the door. If you're gone for days, weeks and months at a time, as your woman, I want to know why. If you got stashes in the house, I want the combination and the keys. Can you deal with that? 'Cause if not, we can chalk this up to a friendship and go about our business."

Sincere paced around my living room. "China, we both have secrets for different reasons. So, if I'm letting you in on everything about me, I want to know all there is to know about you. I peeped your style from day one, and I know you ain't as ignorant to the game as you claim to be. So the question is, are you ready to establish this, or do you want to continue to play me like I'm some nut? And don't give me no half-ass stories, lies and fairy tales. I want to hear it all. And if at any point I find out something different than what you tell me, I feel for you. Don't ever cross me."

Sincere stared at me in silence for a few minutes. "So, before you start talking, make sure you're ready for this. You ain't never seen the side of me that got these niggas out here shook, and I hope it don't ever come down to that."

Now it was China's turn to think. Shit, she could end this mess now. She could forget the fact that this man took something away from me that she cared about, or she could continue on with what she planned on doing, risking the fact that he may find out. She knew what she was getting into. She also knew that Sincere was dead serious about what he wanted from her. What she wasn't so sure of was that she could continue on with this without falling in love with him. As grimy as she wanted to be, deep inside, China was a woman with a deep heart and feelings. Even though he's responsible for Jag's death, a part of her still wanted Sincere, very much.

If China told Sincere about Jag, what will happen to her? If she decided to tell him about Kurt and Blake and Tommy, what would he do? There's only one way to find out. "I figure if I'm honest about it all, then maybe he'd be honest with me about what he's done," she told herself.

"Sincere, look, I've been through a lot. Everything I touch and everyone I love — gone. My father died when I was a little girl. I cut my mother off when I was in college because of her mental, physical and emotional abuse. I met two wonderful friends, Teri and Angie, and they became the family I didn't have. I met a man named Jag, and we hit it off really well."

She looked at him to see his reaction. "We were going to get married, but he was killed. After that, I hit rock bottom. It took me a really long time to snap back, and when I did, I met someone new. His name was Blake. He swept me off my feet from day one. But it wasn't long before he was beating my ass. I ended up pregnant, but I lost the baby. He killed himself. It hasn't been that long since this all happened. The hardest part was testifying in court, but it was worth it in the end when he was handed a life sentence."

"And now," she got quiet, "I've just been trying to rebuild my life since then. I had money stashed away because I knew after Jag that dealing with dudes in this business, anything could happen at any time. So, when I was able to, I moved out here and tried to start over. But my heart still hurts, and I still feel a deep sorrow. There is always something to remind me of my son and the men in my life. So, attachment is extremely hard for me to deal with. I'm afraid to get close to anyone, knowing that one day I could lose them, too."

She wiped her eyes and looked directly at Sincere. She needed to know if she struck a nerve. She wanted to know if he'd confess to what he'd done to Jag or even knowing Kurt. Sincere ran his fingers through my hair.

China
Doll

"Is this why you were crying that night?"

"Yes. You were talking about losing people close to you and not wanting to let anyone in, and it hit me hard. I tried to suppress my feelings, hoping that eventually the hurt would go away, but it doesn't work. I'm not sure if I'll ever be OK. Shit, I'm not sure if I've ever been OK. My life has never been easy. If it's not one thing, it's another. And when things are good, it doesn't last long," she said.

Sincere sat deep in thought for a while.

"China, I know those people you were talking about. I did business with Jag, and I was there the night he was shot."

She looked at him and wondered how she should ask the next question. China began slowly. "Did you have something to do with it?"

"No."

She didn't know if she believed him. She asked another question. "Do you know who did?"

"Some things just don't need to be said, China. Just know that I wasn't the one who pulled the trigger. I wouldn't lie to you about that."

The code of the streets: no snitching. But what if what he knows can give me closure and peace? She didn't ask him any more questions. Asking a million questions will only make things worse.

That night they made their relationship official. Sincere asked her to move in with him. She didn't think I could do it. She wanted her own space and things to call her own.

Surprisingly, they talked a lot about Kurt and Tommy. Sincere told her that Tommy was trying to be down with him, but he wasn't the type of man that Sincere likes to do business with. Sincere told me he heard about Blake and my son through the grapevine, and he hasn't had any contact with Tommy or Kurt since right before all of that went down.

She kept quiet. Her heart began to ache. "I just pray he dies a horrible death," she said, talking to no one in particular.

"Everyone has their day," Sincere said.

165

China
Doll

Chapter Twenty-Three

Nothing Comes Easy

It's been two weeks since Sincere and I started being open about our feelings and I shared everything about my past, China said to herself. Soon, she started having nightmares about Tommy breaking out of jail and coming to kill her. One night, she woke up in the middle of the night covered in sweat, screaming and crying. Sincere calmed her down and reassured her that he will never let anything happen to her.

"Can you please get me a glass of water?" She asked him as she tried to catch her breath from another horrible dream.

Sincere climbed out of bed and walked down to the kitchen. When he returned, he handed her the glass and sat next to her on the bed. "I have to go out of town, China."

"When?"

"Tomorrow. I'm going to Atlanta for a few days. You think you'll be OK until I get back?"

"Yeah, I'll just ask Angie to stay with me. We have some catching up to do anyway."

"All right. Why don't you stay here?" he offered.

"No, I'd rather her not know too much of my business. That's my girl, and I love her, but I've learned my lesson. We'll just stay at my house."

The next evening, she helped Sincere pack his bags, and loved him down before he left.

Later, Angie arrived with her bags at her front door. "I am starving, China. Fix me something to eat," she requested.

"What do you want?"

"Anything." She sat at the table and leafed through a magazine.

China walked into the kitchen and pulled out some ground turkey meat to defrost. Soon, she was seasoning it for the meatloaf. She used her hands to work in all the ingredients, and before she knew it, she became nauseated and ran into the bathroom and promptly threw up.

"Uh-oh, déjà vu!" Angie said from the bathroom door.

Oh, shit! "Shut your mouth." China sat down at the table and put her hand to her head. "What am I going to do?" She asked.

"Get rid of it," she answered in a matter-of-fact tone. China contemplated calling the clinic, but wasn't even sure she was pregnant. One thing for sure, if I'm pregnant, I'm not keeping it.

For three days, she thought about her situation. China could be honest with Sincere, tell him about the baby, or she could lie to Sincere, have the baby and hope for the best on her own. After much debate, she decided to tell Sincere that she was carrying his baby. She devised a plan to make sure he knew exactly how real this was. The night Sincere came back from Atlanta, she drove to meet him and took him out to dinner. she played over her food and skipped her usual cocktail.

"You OK?" he asked.

"I think I'm coming down with something. My appetite has been funny since yesterday. Probably just a cold," she lied.

They drove back to his house.

"I missed you," China told him, pulling him to his bedroom.

"I missed you too, baby."

"Take your clothes off," she demanded. He obeyed.

"Lie down," she said forcefully.

Sincere lay on the bed. He was naked and worth the wait. China stripped down to nothing in front of him and danced her way onto the bed, where she straddled him and kissed him deeply. "I missed you so much," she whispered.

A wave of nausea hit her, and she really felt the need to throw up. Swallowing the rising bile, she moved down and kissed Sincere's chest, stomach and finally, she took his manhood into her mouth. The whole time she was trying hard not to gag. She sucked and flicked the head, moving it up and down in her mouth. She took him in as far as my throat would allow.

Sincere's body jerked, and he grabbed her hair. "You feel so good. I'm ready, baby," he moaned.

Before he could release himself, she climbed on top of him.

"Wait, wait, Daddy. I want more." She guided him into her sweet spot, slowly.

"Oh, shit!" he screamed. "Fuck me, China!"

China moved her body up and down while fondling his balls. This drove him insane! When she felt his body telling her he couldn't take it anymore, she pushed him deeper inside of her.

"Baby, get up, I'm about to come," he panted. She didn't stop. She moved faster and faster like she was riding a bull. He grit his teeth. Still riding him, China sucked on his neck pushing him to the limit.

Finally, Sincere couldn't take anymore. "Boom, boom, boom!" he shouted, coming inside of her.

"Ohhh, Daddy. You filled me up," China purred in his ear. She looked at him to see a smile light up his face. They both began to giggle, and she rolled off him.

"You better hope I don't get used to that," Sincere said, pointing between my legs. "I can see you walking around here with a fat belly, all mean and hungry!" he laughed.

China got up from the bed and walked into the bathroom to run the shower. After almost an hour in the shower, she dried off and lotioned her body. Sincere was already fast asleep, which meant she could get some well-deserved rest.

China woke up the next morning feeling the sun shining on her face. When she rolled over, Sincere wasn't in bed. He stood on the deck talking on his cell phone. She went to the bathroom to brush her teeth and then climbed back in bed waiting for him to finish his call.

"I see you're finally up," he said, kissing her on my forehead.

"Finally? What time is it?" China asked.

"It's almost 1 o'clock."

"In the afternoon?" She couldn't believe that she had slept so long.

"Everything OK? You never sleep this long. You want something to eat? I can have Marisol make us some pancakes and sausage."

China hauled ass to the bathroom and threw up.

"Damn, baby, what you got? A virus? Maybe you should lie back down. I'll get you some juice." Sincere left her on the bathroom floor, hugging the toilet.

She had to get myself together or there's no way to hide this pregnancy until she was ready for Sincere to

China Doll

know. China needed to make an excuse to go home before he started asking questions.

When Sincere returned with a tall glass of juice, China was pulling on her jeans.

"Where are you going?" he asked, setting it on the bedside table.

"Baby, I'm going to go home. I'm not feeling good at all, and I don't want you to get sick. I'm going to call my doctor and see if they can call me something in. I feel horrible."

"Are you sure?" he asked with concern.

"Yeah, I'll call you to let you know I got home, OK?" Once in her car, she hightailed it toward the highway, grabbed her cell phone out of her purse and dialed Angie. "Hey, girl," she answered. "Houston, we have a problem! I'm sick as shit! I can't hold anything down," China yelled into the phone.

"Uh, that would be a symptom of being pregnant, China."

"I know that!" she yelled. "How in the hell am I supposed to hide this for at least four weeks without Sincere realizing what's going on? He is going to kill me!"

"Calm down. Like I said before, you can always get it taken care of. Do you think you're ready for this? I mean, with all that's happened, is this something you really want to do now?"

"Look, there is no way I am getting rid of this baby. Nobody but you and I know that anyway. I have a chance at a new family, and I'm taking it."

China ended her call and rode the rest of the way home thinking about my situation. After she walked inside, she picked up her phone again and dialed the obstetrician.

"Moore OB/GYN, how can I help you?" the receptionist answered.

"Hi, my name is China Doll, and I'd like to make an appointment to see Dr. Moore. I think I may be pregnant,

China
Doll

and I'd like to know for sure."

"OK, Ms. Doll, we have an opening tomorrow morning at nine o'clock."

"That will be fine."

"Please drink plenty of water before you come. The doctor will want to do an ultrasound. Your co-pay will be $40, because this is not your annual visit, and it will be due at the time of your appointment."

"Thank you," she said.

Tomorrow couldn't come fast enough. "Maybe the doctor will tell me that I'm not pregnant and that it's just stress or I have a virus," she hoped

The next morning, she waited for the nurse to call her name in the obstetrician's office. She escorted China into a room where she changed into a paper hospital gown.

"Good morning, China," Dr. Moore greeted her. "I hear that there may be baby number two for you."

"Yes," she said, not offering any further information about the death of my first child.

"OK, if you'll just slide down on the table and place your feet into the stirrups, I'll start your exam."

China did as she was told and watched as Dr. Moore squirted jelly onto his gloved hand. He inserted his fingers into her vagina, pushed down on her stomach and let out a sigh.

"Yup, you're definitely pregnant. I'm going to pull the ultra sound machine in and see exactly how far you are along."

China was conflicted. Am I happy? Am I sad? Am I pissed? I don't know what emotion to feel now, she thought.

The doctor returned and squirted more jelly onto the paddle of a machine and lifted her gown. He placed the paddle on China's belly and moved it around slowly.

"There's your baby." He pointed at the screen, and then he smiled. "I'm going to take some measurements. Do you know the first day of your last period?" he asked.

China
Doll

"I'm not really sure offhand," she admitted.

"That's OK. I can pretty much get an accurate read through the ultrasound."

She saw a small image on the screen and guessed it was her uterus.

"Well, you are about …" he paused to calculate, "I'd say about six weeks pregnant. I'm estimating that your due date is July 19."

The doctor printed out a copy of the ultrasound, and China cleaned up and drove home.

Once there, she sat on my couch staring at the picture of her new baby. She felt overwhelmed with emotion. Her thoughts flew to her first child, and she wondered what he'd be like today. She thought about having two little ones running around driving her crazy, which caused her to start laughing. Then the doorbell rang. China opened the door right away.

"Hey, you OK?" Angie asked.

"Yeah." China walked away from the door leaving it open for her to enter. "I just got back from the doctor." China flopped down on the couch. "I'm definitely pregnant. He said I'm six weeks."

She dialed Sincere's number. He didn't answer, so she left a message for him to call her. Within minutes, her phone was ringing.

"Hey, what's up?" Sincere asked.

"Hey, baby, you think you can come over here? I need to talk to you about something."

"I'm in the middle of something right now. Can I come through in about an hour? I just got to wrap some things up, and then I'll have some time to get out there."

"Yeah, that's fine," she smiled.

China hung up with him and talked to Angie for a while. Soon, Sincere called back to say he was on his way.

"See you later, girl," Angie said smiling as she walked out the door.

China
Doll

China waited, pacing the floor for Sincere to ring the doorbell. It seemed as if it took forever. She found myself smiling, though. It was like a weight had been lifted off her shoulders. Deception is tiring. Nervously, she bit her nails down to the cuticle. Finally, the doorbell rang. Happily, she skipped to the door.

"What's going on? Everything all right?" Sincere asked as he walked into the house.

"Well," she said slowly, smiling, "I went to the doctor this morning, and," she drew out her words, continuing to smile, "he told me that I'm six weeks pregnant."

"For real?" Sincere said. He became quiet.

"Yeah, here's the picture of the baby," she said, handing him the picture from the ultrasound. "What are you doing on July 19?" she asked.

"Why?"

"That's my due date. July 19, Daddy," China smiled. Sincere studied the picture silently.

"Are you upset or just in shock?"

"So this is why you were sick?"

"Yeah, I guess so."

"Well, are you keeping it?" he asked.

"Yes. Of course," she responded. "Don't you want me to keep it?"

"The damage is done," he said.

"I can't believe this shit, Sincere!" she stood up and got in his face. "How can you sit here and say that?" she screamed. "Didn't you take health class? And what about you wanting to see me all pregnant and big?"

He looked at me. "First of all, back the fuck up," he said. "I told you before about talking to me like that. You need to calm down. I've been down this road before, and I know how sheisty some bitches can be."

"Bitches?" China thought she was about to lose her mind. "I asked him to come to my house, and I'm all

174

China
Doll

happy, and now this shit?" she asked herself. "So, after all this time and all the conversations we had, I boil down to one of them hood rat bitches you're used to fucking with?"

Her heart was beating like a tom-tom.

"I have my own shit, Sincere. And if I can remember correctly, I've never asked your black ass for a fucking thing. I don't need a sponsor or someone to take care of me. So, you need to decide if you plan on being a part of this baby's life, or if I should scratch you off as just another deadbeat," she yelled.

Now she was so pissed that she could beat the shit out of him. China crossed her arms and glared at him.

She sat on the floor fuming like a child put in timeout.

"Are you finished?" he asked. China got up off the floor and sat down on the sofa.

"You need to really check yourself, China, for real. You got me all fucked up." Then he walked out of the house. A few minutes later, China stopped crying. She didn't even run after him.

175

*China
Doll*

Chapter Twenty-Four

The Shit Hits the Fan

Three months passed since the day Sincere walked out on China. He called a few times, but, of course, she didn't answer. For what? There is nothing that he can say to change anything. What's done is done, and she's hell-bent on doing this alone.

Her body yearned for sleep, and China found herself sleeping all the time now. In fact, tonight, she was asleep in bed when the phone rang. It was a collect call from prison. The only person she knew in prison was Tommy. Her stomach started to turn, but she was sure there was no way he could get her new phone number.

She'd gotten other collect calls before. Most nights the calls are short and end with a little heavy breathing, nothing too scary. Tonight, however, the person on the other end said nothing at first. Then, the voice ended the call with "dead bitch walking." she slammed down my phone and began to pace the room.

"What am I going to do? I could really use a drink right about now, but I know I shouldn't." She touched her belly.

China was scared shitless. Someone had her phone number, and that meant they probably had her address, too. It had to be Tommy or one of his boys. After all, she didn't have a beef with anyone else. China didn't know anyone else who was locked up. She thought long and hard about what she should do. "Time to get the hell out of Dodge." But where could she go? Sincere. She crossed her fingers and dialed his number.

"Hello," he answered.

"Sincere, I need your help." Her heart was beating fast. "Something is wrong, and I need to meet you at your house," she said frantically.

He paused for what seemed like several minutes. "All right, I'm home, so just come through."

She grabbed what she could, threw it in a bag and flew out the door. When she reached the highway, China realized that she hadn't taken one breath since talking to Sincere. Finally, she exhaled. Breathing deeply, she placed her hand on my stomach. A small baby bump was beginning to appear. China wondered what Sincere would say. When she arrived at his house, he was standing in his driveway.

"What's the problem?"

"He — he's going to kill me!" she shouted.

"What's going on, China? Who's trying to kill you?" Sincere looked confused.

"Tommy!" she screamed.

He pulled her into the house. "Explain."

"Someone has been calling me collect from jail. And the only person I know in jail is Tommy." Tears burst from her eyes. She was so sick of crying, but couldn't help it. "At — at, first, he didn't say anything." She sniffled and hiccupped. "But, but today, he called and said, 'dead bitch walking.' I know it's him, Sincere." she cried, leaning on him.

Sincere wrapped his arms around her. "Listen, you stay with me. You'll be safe here. I'll find out if the streets are talking."

"I need to get out of here. I need to be on a plane. I can't risk something happening to my baby," she said, almost hysterical.

"Calm down, China." Sincere touched her stomach and smiled. He used his thumb to wipe away her tears.

"Let me take care of this."

For two weeks China hid away at Sincere's house. She didn't even tell Angie where she was. Sincere sent Marisol to Puerto Rico to see her mother. She thought it was a vacation, but it was to keep her out of the drama. Sincere figured the fewer people who knew what was going on, the better.

China
Doll

"Listen, I heard some shit. Tommy has a hit on you. The good thing is that nobody knows that we fuck around, so they wouldn't even know to look here. But you can't go back to your house. Word is that he put up some big money for this shit," Sincere said, then he became quiet and serious.

"What!"

"I got a couple of people I can talk to. I'll find out what's really good."

China couldn't speak. She sat down on the step and held her head. The baby moved. This was the first time that happened, but her mind was so preoccupied that she couldn't enjoy the moment.

"China, don't worry. I got you," Sincere said.

"How can I not worry? Someone is trying to kill me. I'm sorry, but I think I have the right to worry," she replied sarcastically. Her mind was reeling and she felt like she was going to be sick.

"Look, I need to leave again. I'll be back soon." He sat next to me. "I'm not going to let anything happen to you." He stood up and walked to the door. "I'm going to see what I can find out. Go on upstairs and rest."

She watched him leave and wondered, "Do I really deserve this bullshit? If he can take care of this shit, I will forever be indebted to him. But will the fear in my heart ever completely go away?"

She lay across Sincere's bed staring at the wall. So many thoughts ran through her mind, but she couldn't focus on one particular thing. Soon, she closed my eyes and began to drift off. A glass shattered, spraying sparkling shrapnel. The sound of the breaking glass jolted her from my sleep. She could barely catch her breath. The house was dark. "Sincere!" she called out, hoping that he dropped a plate in the kitchen. Next, she heard footsteps creeping up the stairs, and China knew it wasn't him. She moved quietly across the bedroom, trying to remember where everything was so that I didn't hurt herself or make any unnecessary noise.

China
Doll

She made it to the closet and crouched down behind a pile of clothes. She had no idea where Sincere kept his guns, so she was powerless. Feeling around, she grabbed one of his shoes, as if the flat heel of a man's shoe is any use against a bullet.

"That bitch is in here somewhere," she heard someone whisper.

Her heart was racing a mile a minute. China was sure whoever was out there could hear the beating or at least hear her breathing. She felt like she would pass out. What am I going to do? How did anyone know I was here? How did they get in? Where's Sincere?

"Yo, check the closet," a voice whispered.

The door opened, and she held her breath. The yellow jaundiced eyes of a large masked killer peered in. Standing just two feet away from her, he used his gun to sift through the clothes. She could smell that he'd been drinking. A many-legged quiver of fear slithered up her back, and she could feel her baby move again. Does the baby know we are mere inches from danger?

"Here she is!" he yelled, his voice scratchy, like someone who smokes three packs a day.

He grabbed her by my hair and dragged her out of the closet. "Yeah, bitch, it's on now!" he yelled, his fingers still tangled in my hair.

"Please," she screamed, hoping it would stop them, "I'm pregnant. Don't hurt my baby!"

"Shut up, bitch!" he bellowed and tossed her across the room.

"Yo, man, this bitch is bad! Let me get that first," the other masked man barked. She could see his pale skin through his mask. He licked his lips with a bright red tongue.

China started to fight. She was not going out without them knowing that she wasn't just any bitch. She knew they could kill her with one shot, but they would have to fight for it! She kicked, screamed and clawed, but her efforts were useless against the force of two burly men.

181

China
Doll

"Bitch, are you crazy?" the pale one backhanded her. She fell back onto the bed and tried to crawl away, almost making it to the bedroom door.

"Get your ass back over here," the drunk one screamed. He grabbed her by the ankles and pulled her across the floor.

She kicked at him and connected with the side of his head.

"Bitch!" he spat at her. "You'll pay for that. Help me," he called to his friend.

They pulled off her sweatpants and ripped off her panties. One of them held her down while the other one spread her legs. Then he shoved his fingers inside her. She howled like a wounded puppy. She yelled out in pain, but they continued on. The man took his fingers out of her cherry spot and licked them, then he leaned down and breathed his hot, funky breath into her ear. "You taste good, bitch." He smiled, and his crooked, rotten teeth were painful to look at.

"Please," she begged, "leave me alone. I have money, but please don't hurt me or my baby."

"Yeah, this is going to be some good-ass pussy!" he said with a lustful smirk on his face. Without another word, he kneeled between her legs, unzipped his jeans and rammed her.

"Fuck her good, man!" The other pervert took off his jacket and unzipped his pants so that he was ready when it was his turn.

China screamed bloody murder.

"Shut this bitch up!" the one yelled to his friend.

He clapped his rough hands over her mouth. The stench on his skin almost made her vomit. She used all her strength to move her body back and forth so that he had to get off her. But her movements seemed to turn the beast on even more.

"Hurry up, man!" the one covering her mouth shouted through his thin lips. "I want my turn."

Every thrust he made sent pain shooting through her body. "If I live, would I ever enjoy sex again?" she wondered.

She felt his body jerk. The bastard's once-stiff penis was now a limp log stuck to the side of her leg.

She was trembling. Where's Sincere? Tears rolled down her face and puddled beside her ears. He promised me he wouldn't let anything happen to me, and now this. And it's happening right in his house.

"Get up, man. It's my turn." They switched places.

"Let me get some of that," he said. His jack-rabbit movements were making her nauseous.

She jerked and almost threw up.

His eyes were deep wells with foul water glistening darkly at the bottom. "Man, this bitch is about to throw

China Doll

up." He looked at his friend whose hand was covering her mouth. "Bitch, you better not throw up on me," he warned her.

Despite her sickness, he didn't stop.

His breathing was labored, and his filthy sweat dripped on her. Then his moans grew louder. "Oh, yeah, oh, yeah, oh, yeah, baby!"

Before he could bust a nut, Sincere burst into the room.

"What the fuck!" he screamed.

Both men looked in his direction. The one inside her stumbled over himself to pull up his pants, and his friend rolled off the bed and onto the floor. The sound of gunfire filled her ears. Sparks from the nozzle of the gun sprayed out into the dark room.

"Get down, China!" Sincere screamed. He ducked behind the bathroom door and continued to fire his pistol at the two rapists.

China rolled off the bed in the opposite direction and crawled under it.

"Fuck!" one of them screamed. "I'm hit! I'm hit!" he kept hollering in pain. The other one continued to fire at Sincere.

China curled into a ball under the bed. She could see the legs of the man that Sincere shot. He was lying on the floor, writhing in pain, whimpering. She was so glad that he was punished for the pain he caused. The sound of gunfire traveled into the hallway.

"Motherfucker!" Sincere bellowed. "Don't you ever come into my motherfucking house!"

Next came the sound of a body rolling down the steps, and finally, all gunfire stopped. The silence was even more deafening. Seconds, minutes, hours seemed to pass.

"China," Sincere called, "China, are you all right?" He helped her climb out from under the bed.

"Sincere." she hiccupped. "Sincere, baby." Shuddering, she cried into his shirt, grabbing, clawing at his clothes.

She was terrified. What was going to happen to her next? Her tears turned into hysteria. She was unable to tell him exactly what happened, when, or why. Her clothes were disheveled and blood poured from her lip and nose. As China stood, she felt liquid — blood or come, she didn't know — seeping down from between her legs.

"Are you OK, baby?" he asked.

She couldn't speak. Tears fell from her eyes like water from a hose.

"Let me help clean you up." Sincere moved away, but she clutched him.

"Please, please," he begged, not wanting him to leave her for fear that a repeat performance would take place.

They sat on the bed and Sincere pulled out his cell phone. He called someone over to remove the two dead men in the house. China zoned out, and flashbacks of the traumatic ordeal consumed her. She heard their voices and smelled their odors.

"Do you want to go to the hospital?" Sincere asked.

"No," is all she could say. She was worried about her baby and couldn't move.

"Come with me to the bathroom."

Slowly, she rose and walked with Sincere to the bathroom. He ran a rag under the cold water and dabbed at the bruises that began to form at her temple and on her jaw. She flinched, and his movements became even more tender. Sweat beaded her brow, and he blotted her face with a towel. Once he cleaned her up, he took a clean sweatsuit from his closet, dressed her and put her sneakers on. Gently, he finger combed her hair and helped her down the stairs. The sight of the dead man at the bottom of the steps made China whimper louder.

"He's not going to hurt you again, baby," Sincere told her.

He helped her into the car and peeled out of the driveway. She wanted to ask where they were going, but before she could think to say anything, she closed her eyes

184

China
Doll

and drifted off.

"Baby, baby?"

Sincere's voice rocked her from sleep.

"China, I'm going to check us into a hotel out in DC"

She nodded her head and continued to sit in silence. Sincere placed his hand over hers. "I'm sorry I wasn't there."

She tried to smile. She felt so numb.

They pulled up to the Wyndham Hotel. Sincere checked in, and they headed to the room.

"I'm going to run you a bath, OK?" Sincere offered. China nodded

The hot water stung all the sensitive spots, causing her to flinch and move around, struggling to find a comfortable position. Sincere sat on the edge of the tub sponging soapy water on her.

"Baby, I'm so sorry," he said.

He was visibly upset. "It's not your fault, baby."

Eventually, the warm water made her relax. By now, she had stopped crying. China just needed to rest.

"I wish I would have never left you alone. I wish I could kill them niggas again." He jumped up as if he were preparing to go to war all over again.

"Sincere," she called to him, wanting to calm him down, "Give me your hand."

China pulled his hand down to her tummy. "The baby is moving." He gently held his hand on her belly.

"I don't think I feel anything."

"It's just small flutters," she said, smiling up at him. China could tell he was still conflicted, but he cracked a tiny smile.

She stayed in the bathtub a little while longer. Her mind jumped from one thing to the next. How did she get there? What did she do to deserve this?

"Thank you," she said to Sincere as she got dressed.

"What?" Sincere asked. He was concentrating on something on his cell.

"Thank you. Sincere, if it wasn't for you, I'd be dead right now. And please don't blame yourself. You've been taking care and watching out for me for weeks now. It's not your fault. Really."

"If I would have stayed with you, this wouldn't have happened. All I can picture right now is that nigga on top of you, and it's killing me. I hate to be selfish, because I know how you feel right now, but I'm hurting. I should have been able to protect you," Sincere said.

China walked over to him and massaged his head, trying to comfort him as best as she could. He stayed up all night, holding her, touching my belly and assuring her that everything would be OK. She couldn't sleep either, despite the fact that she was tired as hell. All she could think of is that she could really be dead right now. If those broke-down criminals could find her, then shit, anyone could. How long can I hide out? Something has to happen. China needed to know that I was going to be safe. That her baby would be safe. How can I bring another child into this world under the same circumstances?

"Sincere?"

"Yeah, babe," he answered.

"I'm never going to be safe, am I?"

He didn't say anything. She wondered if he was thinking about his promise to keep her safe and then she got raped right in his house.

"We have to do something about Tommy. He's the root of this problem. Until he's taken care of, my life will always be in his hands," China stated.

"I was just thinking about that. Let me handle it. I don't want you worrying about anything."

She closed her eyes and tried to find relief in his words. It's ironic how the man I planned to set up to kill Kurt

186

China
Doll

would end up doing it willingly for me anyway. Maybe it wasn't by chance that Sincere crossed my path after all.

Soon, she could hear Sincere on the phone. Did China really want to know what he was talking about?

He dialed another number. "Yo, what's up? I need you to meet me at the Wyndham Hotel in D.C." He hung up and walked over to her.

"China, I'm going to meet Young Trap to discuss some things. Hasan is coming here to look after you. Do not let him in this room. He is to sit outside the door to make sure don't nothing go down. I'll write down his cell phone number." He scribbled on the pad next to the bed. "If you need him, you call him from the hotel phone. If something happens, he'll be right outside the door. I'll give him my key. He's my man, and I trust him, so I know he's going to take care of you." He pulled on his jacket.

"When are you coming back?" She asked. She was nervous that he was leaving.

China
Doll

"I won't be long. If you need me just call me. I'll call to check on you, and I'll make sure I call to let you know when I'm on my way back. Call Room Service."

"I'm not hungry."

"Yeah, but you need to eat. You need to feed my baby."

"Your baby?" It's amazing what rape and a near-death experience can change.

Outside the room China heard Sincere talking to someone. Must be Hasan. She peeked out the peephole and saw a massive man outside the door. He resembled a gorilla.

For two hours she picked over my breakfast. The baby finally calmed down, which gave her a little more relief. Those tiny flutters were beginning to get on her nerves. She wanted to call Angie to let her know what happened, but she figured the fewer people who know where she was, the better. China didn't trust anyone. Not even Angie. Especially now, she felt all alone all over again. She was grateful that Sincere was riding this one out with her, but she wasn't so sure he could fix this. "What if someone comes at him? Who will I be left with? Who will protect me then?" she thought.

The hotel phone rang. China jumped, not sure who it could be. Then she remembered Sincere said he'd call on the hotel phone.

"Hello."

"Baby, you OK?" Sincere asked.

"Yeah, just waiting for you to get back," China said.

"I'm on my way now. I should be there in about 20 minutes. Is Hasan still outside the door?"

"Yeah, he's still out here."

"Good. I'll see you in a few minutes."

Not long after the phone call, Sincere entered the room.

"Hey, everything OK?"

"Yes, is Hasan gone?" She wanted to know.

"Yeah, he just left. I talked to Trap and let him know what's going on. I think we're ready to take care of this."

Sincere told her how Young Trap, a good friend from back in the day, agreed to get set up with some drugs. He's on parole, so once he gets picked up, he'll go to Western Correctional Institution. If everything goes as planned, Trap will have easy access to Tommy.

"He's willing to sacrifice his freedom for me?" She asked, baffled by this guy's loyalty.

"He'll do it for me," Sincere replied.

She still couldn't understand it. But if it works, that's all she was concerned about. There are some things in life you'll never understand.

"So when is all this supposed to go down?"

"Tonight."

"That fast?"

"The sooner we do this, the better. We can't waste no time. This nigga Tommy almost took something very important away from me. And in doing so, he caused you pain. He can't live no more. Ain't nobody going to fuck with mine," Sincere banged on his chest, "and live to see another day. Once Trap gets processed, he's going to call me to let me know shit is good. Once that happens, it's only a matter of time before he gets at Tommy.

"And I found out them young boys that did that to you was some niggas from Brooklyn. I'm putting a call in to my peoples and let them know that they overstepped their bounds. So, it's either going to be an all-out war, or those motherfuckers is going to fall back. They really don't want it with me. I supply too much of their shit down here. And I know they ain't ready to fuck up business over some bullshit-ass jailbird."

"Tommy ain't down with nobody like that anyway. He just had the right amount of money at the right time. I'm sure he ain't say who he was fucking with, 'cause if my peoples up there would have known he was coming to where I rest my head at, it never would have popped off." Sincere was hyped. He began pacing the room and sweating.

China Doll

👑 👑 👑 👑 👑 👑 👑 👑 👑 👑 👑 👑 👑 👑 👑 👑

For three days China waited anxiously for the call. She didn't know how long it would take for Trap to get locked up and processed, but she damn sure wished it would finally happen. On the sixth day, Sincere's cell phone went off. He jumped from his sleep to answer it. As with all his calls, China held her breath and listened to see if it was Trap.

"What's up?" Sincere said. He listened.

"Naw, man, them bitch-ass niggas ran up in my shit, raped my girl and violated!" Sincere stood up and paced the floor. "You know me better than that! Fuck that. I don't give a fuck who they were," he screamed into the phone. He continued to pace as he listened intently.

"You ready for war, nigga, or are you about making this money? I can go either way. Now, if those niggas was more important than what we trying to do, then you let me know. I'm ready to strap up as we speak!" he screamed.

China worried others in the hotel would hear him. Not sure what was going to happen next, she sat still. Finally, Sincere hung up.

"Now what?" She asked nervously.

"Now I go back to making my money. Tommy is fucked. If Trap don't get at him, he's still dead. Them niggas ain't ready for what I got. They ain't ready to start no shit over some small-time niggas." He walked over to look out the window. The curtains had been closed for days.

Sincere's cell phone rang again. "Yo," he hollered into the phone. "Where you at?"

China studied the expression on his face, but couldn't tell what he was feeling. Sincere has the ultimate poker face. "All right, sit tight. You got bail? All right, call me and let me know what's good."

He turned to China. "Listen, I'm going to make sure you good. One." Sincere hung up the phone and kissed her on the forehead. "We're good. They got Trap. That was his one phone call. They're not giving him bail. They're going to ship him to Western first thing in the morning."

China's heart started racing. The baby started moving again.

"So now what? We just wait?"

"Yeah, that's all we can do right now. Once it's done, if he don't get caught, he'll call to let me know. He's going to put Hasan on his visiting list in the meantime, so that if he does get caught, Hasan can go to see him. If they say Trap can't get no visits, that means he's in segregation, and that means the job done," Sincere informed me.

Each day that passed China grew more and more anxious. She was always sick to her stomach and couldn't keep anything down. By the following week, she damn

*China
Doll*

near pulled her hair out. Trap called Sincere every day to check in. Each time he called, China stopped breathing, hoping that he had done what he was supposed to. And each time she was let down when Sincere broke the bad news.

Two more weeks passed, and Sincere got his daily call from Trap.

"Yo, nigga, what's up?" Sincere asked. He put him on speakerphone so China could hear.

"Chilling, dawg. They got me on cleanup duty. I just got finished not that long ago," Trap said.

"Word? I hope that shit ain't too messy," Sincere said in code.

She learned the code weeks ago.

"Naw, dawg, that shit ain't take no time at all. I did what I had to do, and now I'm chilling. But on some other shit, I'm going to need you to put some dough on my books. A nigga is hungry," Trap said.

"Yeah, I got you. Stay in touch and let me know if there's anything else I can do. Are they saying how long you got?" Sincere asked.

"I'm waiting to hear back from my lawyer now. He's supposed to come see me tomorrow. Looks like when they brought me in, they didn't follow proper procedure. My paperwork is all fucked-up, so it looks like I may be home on a technicality. I'll be in touch though."

Sincere ended the call. He was smiling from ear to ear.

"It's done, baby."

"Finally! So can we go home now?" China asked. She didn't think it could happen, but she was actually tired of living in this hotel. Plus, she needed to get to the doctor.

"Let's stay here for a few more days, and then we can bounce," he said.

At the end of the week China was packing up all the things that they'd accumulated. "I am so happy to be going home," she said.

But when they pulled up to the house, the memory of the night of the rape hit her like a ton of bricks. That night had become a memory, but now it was a harsh reality. She wasn't sure she could stay here. "I don't know, Sincere," she said, hesitating before getting out of the car. Not only did she not want to stay there, but she didn't want to go to her house either. She felt homeless.

"What's wrong?" Sincere asked.

"I can't go in there. I can't sleep in that bed. I thought I was OK, but I can't do it," she said, staring at the house. Sincere sighed.

"What you want to do? You want to go home?"

"No, I can't go there either. I guess I have to get a room somewhere until I find a new spot," China said, sure as hell not wanting to go back to a hotel. But what other choice did she have?

"Well, I'm not leaving you alone. Let me just grab a few things. You can wait in the car," he said.

She sat in the car and waited patiently for Sincere to return. Soon, she closed her eyes to pass the time and fell asleep. Suddenly, something startled her out of her sleep. She checked her watch and realized that Sincere had been gone for a while. She started to worry. She called his cell phone, but no answer.

Go inside, her mind screamed, but she couldn't do it. She waited for another 15 minutes, still no sign of Sincere. She rubbed my growing belly and took a deep breath and hesitantly got out of the car and looked around. Nothing looks out of place. With each step toward the house, her legs grew heavier. When she got to the door, she called Sincere's name. He didn't answer.

Cautiously, China walked inside and called his name again. She pictured the guy lying at the bottom of the steps, and hesitated. Nausea gripped her stomach, but she quelled the desire to vomit. Slowly, she walked upstairs and into the bedroom. No sign of Sincere. Two men stood in the room, and China started to tremble. She started to

China
Doll

whirl around, desperate to leave the house, then out of nowhere, someone grabbed her from behind.

"Shit!" she screamed, and began to cry. "Don't hurt me!" She begged.

"Calm down," Sincere said.

"What the fuck!" She screamed at him, slugging him in the arm. "You scared the shit out of me! Didn't you hear me calling you?" China asked, leaning over, trying to catch her breath.

"No, I was in the basement." He picked up a bag, and they began to walk down the stairs.

"I called your cell phone!" she yelled, trying to explain to him how hard she tried to get in touch with him.

"China, I was in the basement. It's OK. I don't get reception down there. Come on, let me get you out of here."

They reached the middle of the foyer and the lights went out.

"Did you pay the bill?" She asked, grabbing his arm.

Sincere ignored her and pulled her closer. He placed his finger over her mouth. They tiptoed toward the front door, but before they could open it, shots were fired through the windows.

China
Doll

"Shhh, get down. Crawl to the basement," he whispered.

China did as she was told. She closed the basement door behind her and ran to the far side of the room and hid behind the sectional couch.

"I must be fucking dreaming. I can't go through this shit again."

She heard gunshots and niggas screaming. Tears filled her eyes as she prayed that Sincere was OK. Minutes passed without any noise. She tried to remain calm, but horrible, frightening thoughts consumed her mind. Abruptly, the basement door flew open.

China knew that they were coming to get her, so she curled herself tighter into a ball and prayed that she would just disappear. Footsteps came closer and closer.

"China!"

Finally I was able to breathe again. It was Sincere. She popped up. "I'm over here."

"Come on." He held out his hand. "Let's get the fuck out of here."

They bounded up the steps two at a time. Quickly, they ran and got into the car and sped off and never looked back. She didn't ever want to see that house again.

"What the fuck was that?" she asked, my voice quivering.

"This shit ain't over. I don't know what happened. I need to get in touch with Hasan to have him go up to see Trap. Something ain't right. I think I'm being set up."

China
Doll

Chapter Twenty-Five

Last Stand

"What the fuck?!" China yelled.

"Wake up, China. You must be having a bad dream again."

The hotel phone rang, and Sincere reached for it. "All right, I'm coming down now," he said.

China was hyperventilating. Quickly she got out of bed and went into the bathroom to splash some water on her face. That shit was all too real.

"I'll be back," Sincere said and left the room.

He returned shortly and plopped himself down on the bed. Then he grabbed his cell and began to thumb through his contacts.

"What's wrong?" she asked him, picking up a bottle

of orange juice.

"That nigga crossed me. Trap turned State. He gave up all my spots, my connect, everything. He bailed out last night," Sincere said.

"Do you think he had something to do with what happened last night?" she asked.

"I don't know, but I plan on finding out. I know one thing — we have to get out of this hotel. Even though I think Hasan is the only one who knows we're here, I still don't trust it. Throw something on and let's go," Sincere commanded. China listened.

She was tired. All this dipping and dodging and running was taking its toll on her. She barely ate. Sleep is a medley of nightmares. How long are we going to do this? The news was on, and the word "homicide" caught her attention. She turned it up. Reporters stood outside of Angie's house. They described how her house was broken into and how she was badly beaten and then killed execution style.

"Oh my God!" China screamed and sank to the floor.

"What?" Sincere said coming out of the bathroom. He listened to the tail end of the report. "Your friend?" he asked.

"Angie," China said, unable to make eye contact. "They were trying to find me. I just know it. This is all my fault."

She sat down on the edge of the bed. Angie had no idea how to find her. "If only I would have called her, warned her — something — she'd still be here now."

"Where's my phone?" China asked.

She frantically searched for it, found it, and turned it on. It had been off since the day she got that last collect call. China checked her messages. Several were from Angie, asking where she was and to please call her. She was trying to find China. She said she was worried because she hadn't heard from her. The last message was not one of concern but of terror.

"Listen to this," China said to Sincere. She turned the phone to speaker.

"China! Please call me! Tell me where you are. They're going to kill me! They're going to kill me, China!" she screamed.

She looked at him as she deleted the call. The date of the message was from the night before. It took only a moment before China put two and two together.

She looked at Sincere. "Angie must have told them that we're together. Her last message was last night. That's why they shot up your house," she cried. Her vivid imagination painted a tableau of rape and torture of her best friend.

Sincere sat on the edge of the bed with his head in his hands. "All right, we need to get out of here."

In the car, Sincere broke the silence, and China's thoughts. He was thinking out loud. "Trap turned State's, Tommy is still alive, and I have a feeling those Brooklyn cats have something to do with it, too. They're killing two birds with one stone. Tommy wants you, and my peoples in Brooklyn want me out. It's time for war."

Instead of getting a room in a plush hotel, they opted for a small room in a small motel outside of the city. Sincere contacted his people in Brooklyn and set up a meeting for the next night. He has connects at a pool hall in the city, and it would be closed for the night.

"China, you're going to have to ride with me. I need you there," Sincere said, handing her one of his guns. "Do you know how to shoot?"

China nodded her head yes and took the gun in her hand.

Sincere ran down his plan to me. "We're going to be all right," he assured me. "Everything will be OK."

China wasn't so sure. Sincere was counting on her to be his backup. She was never the little gutter girl used to being the Bonnie to someone's Clyde, but she'd handled guns before. She had to be up for her job – there was no

197

China
Doll

turning back now. It's either ride with her man or give up and accept death. Fuck that, I'm fighting before I go down that way.

We parked out front and saw a black-on-black Cadillac parked near the door of the pool hall. Before we got out of the car, China secured the gun that Sincere gave her into the back of her pants.

"Let's go, baby." Sincere kissed her softly on the lips as if it was going to be the last time he would do it.

They got out of the car and three men exited the Cadillac. Another man, who China assumed was a bodyguard, got out of the driver's side. It's all or nothing now. They all walked into the pool hall and took seats at one of the tables. Her eyes swept across the room.

"What's up, Ike?" Sincere said, acknowledging the older man.

"I'm good, Sincere. I wish I could say the same for you," Ike responded, studying him. Sincere spoke to the other two men. He then introduced China and then business began. "Look, shit is getting hot, as I'm sure all of you know. We've been doing business for many years now, and I'm only talking to you out of respect. I'm outta the game. I'm on a plane tomorrow morning. I'm prepared to turn over my business to your organization," Sincere said.

"Well, I'm sure you understand that it's going to cost you. A lot of profit is at stake with your departure. And we are well aware of your situation, so we also know that sooner than later, you won't have much of a business to offer us," Ike spoke up.

"With all due respect, Ike, I've built one of the most lucrative organizations on the East Coast. It's going to take more than some snitch-ass nigga turning State for them to shut me down just like that." Sincere snapped his fingers to punctuate his point. He looked around and continued talking. "I have investments in areas no one knows about, including you. I'm sure that those things will be of interest

China
Doll

to you," he finished.

The room was so hot. By now, China was sweating and finding it hard to pay attention. She hadn't eaten much that day, and her head began to ache. Surely a ride-or-die bitch would be much more attentive, but she was dealing with some extenuating circumstances.

"Investments ... such as?" Ike asked, his interest piqued.

"Ike, I own half of this city. You want it — it's yours. All I'm asking is to be able to get on that plane tomorrow with my girl and not have to worry about this shit no more," Sincere explained.

The room was quiet. The players in this game exchanged explosive stares that shouted volumes. A bottle behind the bar dropped as if it were China's cue. She made her move and leaned in close to Sincere to whisper in his ear.

"Excuse my girl. She needs to use the ladies' room. If you haven't noticed, she's seven months pregnant," Sincere said, pointing to her bulging belly.

The men nodded in unison, excusing her.

China
Doll

Once inside the bathroom, she closed the door securely behind her. Carefully, China pulled the gun from her waistband and took a deep breath. The bathroom was positioned where no one could see her. She twirled on the silencer and breathed deeply.

Everything had led up to this point, and China was the only line between getting out and getting shot. She needed to make this bullet count. If she missed, they were both dead. She had one chance.

China counted to three and eased out of the bathroom. Cautiously, she peeked around the corner and aimed for Ike. She fired one clean shot and caught him right in the middle of his forehead. Blood spattered everywhere. The other men at the table didn't even know what they were in for.

Before the men at the table could make a move,

Sincere grabbed the gun out of the small of his back and fired quickly at the other two men. They didn't even have a chance to blink. "Motherfucker! This will teach you to fuck with Sincere!" he shouted at them as they fell to the floor.

He turned, quickly aiming at the bodyguard. The bodyguard slipped around a corner, and Sincere turned the table over to duck behind it.

"China!" He yelled, "Get down!"

She turned the corner and took shelter behind some shelves. As soon as China got down, she heard something creak behind her.

"You think you're getting out of here, little bitch?" the bodyguard snarled. "You think you can just get out scott free? You must be dumber than you look." He raised his gun and aimed the barrel at her forehead.

Just as his finger started squeezing the trigger, Sincere appeared right behind him and put his gun up to the bodyguard's temple. I closed my eyes. BOOM. When she opened her eyes again, the wall was covered in blood, skull and brain.

China
Doll

"Bitch please," Sincere quipped, then brushed some skull off of his shoulder. "Let's go," he said, as he picked China up from the ground.

She tucked her gun back into her waistband and wiped the sweat off of her face.

"Are you OK, baby?" He asked. China's adrenaline was pumping so fast. He put his arm around her and they ran to the door and out of the building.

"We'll talk about it later. Let's go."

As they were about to jump into their car, someone appeared from behind the Cadillac.

"Sincere."

"Motherfucker," Sincere winced. He stopped dead in his tracks and squared off with the figure that was just stepping into the car lights. It was Sincere's own boy

– Trap. "I ought to blow your motherfucking head off," Sincere said calmly. "You want to know who shot Jag? He's standing right in front of you, China." Trap nodded.

China's stomach dropped as memories of her first love flashed through my mind. Her knees got weak, but she was too angry to cry. She wanted to kill this motherfucker who shot Jag, and now threatened the father of her unborn child.

"Sincere, come on, baby. Let's go. Let's get out of here," China begged him, pulling him toward the car.

"No. I gotta handle this business now." He looked back toward his old friend. "Trap, I knew you had something to do with this, you grimy-ass nigga!" Sincere spat. "After everything I did for you, this is what it comes down to?"

"Fuck you, motherfucker, I'm trying to eat! This is business, nigga," Trap retorted.

"I always took care of you, Trap. You know that."

"It's time for me to take care of me, and with you out of the game, it's all me."

"You think you're hot shit, don't you?" Sincere took a step toward Trap.

"You better step back, Sincere, I got a clip with your name on every shell." Sincere took a step back and looked at China.

"Come here baby," Sincere held his hand out to China. She walked over to Sincere and he put his arm around her. "You gonna shoot me? Shoot me in front of China?" He put his hand on her stomach. "Shoot me in front of my child?"

Trap spat in his direction. "What's done is done. You know I can't let you just walk away." The two men stood across from each other, the barrel of their guns ready to end each other's lives.

"Go back to the car," Sincere told China. "Time for me to handle this business."

Before she could take a step, she heard shots fire. She tried to run, but a burning sensation in her leg made her drop to the ground.

"Sincere!" China called out.

She saw the faces of Jag, Blake, Angie, Teri, and Tommy flash before her.

"China! Get out of here" Sincere screamed.

He let off shots in Trap's direction. Trap was shooting from behind the car. "Fuck you, nigga!" he screamed.

Sincere grabbed China's arm, still shooting. "Come on, baby. Get up." He tried to smile at her. "You're my girl. I need you, girl." He pulled her to her feet.

She winced in pain. "Sincere, baby," she cried.

"I got you, baby. Just hold on." Sincere pulled the trigger again ¬– and again – and again – then, nothing. He was out of rounds. China pulled my gun and aimed in Trap's direction, popping off round after round blindly into the night air. She kept squeezing the trigger until she was tapped out, too.

"Sincere."

They both stopped, frozen. She could hear her heart beating in her ears. Trap's laughter echoed off the empty buildings. He stepped out from behind the Cadillac, holding his arm. China had hit him with one of her shots, and he was bleeding, badly. He limped slowly toward them.

"You were always the man, Sincere. You had it all. You had the money, the cars – you had whatever you wanted, whenever you wanted it. You even had some bitch to clean your house for you, and you never cut me in. I was living on scraps."

"That's the game, Trap. You knew what you were getting into."

"You're right. I did know. And now it's my time. Sincere ain't controlling the game no more." Trap reached into his jacket and pulled out another clip, slapped it into his piece and aimed at Sincere again. Trap was hurt, but he was still standing. He knew, like they did, that he didn't have much time left.

"Trap, you ain't getting out of here alive. I know it and you know it. Let's work something out. Let me out of the game. I'll disappear."

"Bitch you know it don't work that way." He took another step toward us and spat blood from his mouth, wiping his chin with his jacket sleeve.

"Ain't nobody getting out of here."

Just then, they heard faint sirens as dim red and blue reflections lit up the night. The cops would be there in minutes.

"Looks like we're not alone."

"We still have time to get out of here!" China screamed.

"Shut that bitch up," Trap said with clenched teeth. "She ain't been nothing but trouble since the beginning!"

Just then, a helicopter appeared overhead, shining its search light on all three of them. A voice boomed from the speaker.

"Put the gun down. This is the police. Put your weapons down!"

China Doll

Trap shielded his eyes from the brightness of the lights and the sudden wind. China took a step back, and felt the pain shoot through my leg where she was shot. She looked down and saw a trail of blood from where she was crouched behind the car. The sight of so much blood made her lose my balance, and she stumbled backward and fell to the ground again – the only thing she heard was Sincere calling her name.

"China!" He bellowed. Then, a flurry of gunshots. Trap emptied his remaining clip into both of them. Sincere fell down beside China in a heap, and the police chopper opened fire on Trap from above. He crumpled to the ground, ten feet away from China and Sincere, steaming in the cold night air.

All of the sudden, Sincere grabbed China's hand.

"I love you, girl," he said in a raspy voice, gasping for his last breath.

The last thing she saw was one tear fall from his eye and splash against the pavement.

It was over.

*China
Doll*

Epilogue

And now we turn to the local news. We have Merideth Mathis standing by in downtown Brooklyn. Merideth?

"This is Merideth Mathis, and this is a Breaking News Report. Tonight, shots were reported being fired at Sal's Pool Hall here in Brooklyn. When police arrived at the scene, they found a bloodbath. The victims of tonight's tragedy have not been identified, but at least five males and one pregnant female were involved. Police have no suspects at this time. We'll report more as we get additional information."

China's mother turned off her television and smiled.

♛ Triple Crown Publications

Order Form
P.O. Box 247378 Columbus, OH 43224

Name	
Address	
City	
State	Zipcode

QTY	TITLES	PRICE
	A Down Chick	$15.00
	A Hood Legend	$15.00
	A Hustler's Son	$15.00
	A Hustler's Wife	$15.00
	A Project Chick	$15.00
	Always a Queen	$15.00
	Amongst Thieves	$15.00
	Baby Girl	$15.00
	Baby Girl Pt. 2	$15.00
	Betrayed	$15.00
	Black	$15.00
	Black and Ugly	$15.00
	Blinded	$15.00
	Cash Money	$15.00
	Chances	$15.00
	China Doll	$15.00

Shipping & Handling
1 - 3 Books $5.00
4 - 9 Books $9.00
$1.95 for each add'l book

Total $_____

Forms of accepted payment: Postage Stamps, Personal or Institutional Checks &
Money Orders. All mail in orders take 5-7 business days to be delivered.

♚ Triple Crown Publications

Order Form
P.O. Box 247378 Columbus, OH 43224

Name	
Address	
City	
State	Zipcode

QTY	TITLES	PRICE
	Chyna Black	$15.00
	Contagious	$15.00
	Crack Head	$15.00
	Crack Head II	$15.00
	Cream	$15.00
	Cut Throat	$15.00
	Dangerous	$15.00
	Dime Piece	$15.00
	Dirtier Than Ever	$20.00
	Dirty Red	$15.00
	Dirty South	$15.00
	Diva	$15.00
	Dollar Bill	$15.00
	Ecstasy	$15.00
	Flipside of the Game	$15.00
	For the Strength of You	$15.00

Shipping & Handling
1 - 3 Books $5.00
4 - 9 Books $9.00
$1.95 for each add'l book

Total $_____

Forms of accepted payment: Postage Stamps, Personal or Institutional Checks &
Money Orders. All mail in orders take 5-7 business days to be delivered.

♛ Triple Crown Publications

Order Form

P.O. Box 247378   Columbus, OH 43224

Name	
Address	
City	
State	Zipcode

QTY	TITLES	PRICE
	Game Over	$15.00
	Gangsta	$15.00
	Grimey	$15.00
	Hold U Down	$15.00
	Hood Richest	$15.00
	Hoodwinked	$15.00
	How to Succeed in the Publishing Game	$15.00
	Ice	$15.00
	Imagine This	$15.00
	In Cahootz	$15.00
	Innocent	$15.00
	Karma	$15.00
	Karma II	$15.00
	Keisha	$15.00
	Larceny	$15.00
	Let That Be the Reason	$15.00

Shipping & Handling
1 - 3 Books $5.00
4 - 9 Books $9.00
$1.95 for each add'l book

Total $_____

♔ Triple Crown Publications

Order Form
P.O. Box 247378   Columbus, OH 43224

Name	
Address	
City	
State	Zipcode

QTY	TITLES	PRICE
	Life	$15.00
	Love & Loyalty	$15.00
	Me & My Boyfriend	$15.00
	Menage's Way	$15.00
	Mina's Joint	$15.00
	Mistress of the Game	$15.00
	Queen	$15.00
	Rage Times Fury	$15.00
	Road Dawgz	$15.00
	Sheisty	$15.00
	Stacy	$15.00
	Stained Cotton	$15.00
	Still Dirty	$20.00
	Still Sheisty	$15.00
	Street Love	$15.00
	Sunshine & Rain	$15.00

Shipping & Handling
1 - 3 Books $5.00
4 - 9 Books $9.00
$1.95 for each add'l book

Total $_____

Forms of accepted payment: Postage Stamps, Personal or Institutional Checks & Money Orders. All mail in orders take 5-7 business days to be delivered.

☖Triple Crown Publications

Order Form

P.O. Box 247378   Columbus, OH 43224

Name	
Address	
City	
State	Zipcode

QTY	TITLES	PRICE
	The Cartel's Daughter	$15.00
	The Game	$15.00
	The Hood Rats	$15.00
	The Pink Palace	$15.00
	The Reason Why	$15.00
	The Set Up	$15.00
	Torn	$15.00
	Trickery	$15.00
	Vixen Icon	$15.00
	Whore	$15.00

Shipping & Handling
1 - 3 Books $5.00
4 - 9 Books $9.00
$1.95 for each add'l book

Total $_____